The Magic Phonograph

Short Stories

by

Anthony Stern

FOR MRS. BOTTOMLEY
WITH THE COMPLIMENTS OF THE AUTHOR...

[signature: Anthony Stern]

P.S. AS YOU CAN SEE I <u>DID</u> SUCCEED IN FINDING
SOMEONE TO WRITE THE FOREWORD!

Hope you enjoy the stories.

The Magic Phonograph

Short Stories

by

Anthony Stern

THE PENTLAND PRESS LTD
Edinburgh Cambridge Durham USA

Published by
The Pentland Press Ltd
1 Hutton Close
South Church
Bishop Auckland
Durham

ISBN : 1 85821 810 1

Typeset, printed and bound
by Lintons Printers, Crook, County Durham

*For Guy and Raphael
from Daddy*

Contents

Foreword

In an age dominated so completely by television, it is a great delight occasionally to switch one's 'mode of input' and experience events vicariously through written description.

Short stories are a special technique of enabling others to share a briefly contrived fantasy through the medium of rich and evocative language - upon which we may also project our personal conceptions and experiences.

Anthony presents an interesting scenario, pregnant with possibilities, takes us plausibly through a set of events, and then surprises us. There is of course a skill in this process, and it is one in which Anthony excels.

His encyclopaedic knowledge of many diverse fields is revealed in the stories. They have a ring of truth about them - the descriptions, the terminology, the casual lines - so that we are eased rapidly and effortlessly into the temporary world where the story takes us.

I respect Anthony's skills as a wordsmith and imaginator. Enjoy the stories!

Dr Keith Hearne, B.Sc., M.Sc., Ph.D.
Egham, Surrey, 2000

Dr Keith Hearne is an internationally known psychologist recognised for his pioneering work into lucid dreams and his invention of the Dream Machine. He is frequently on television, radio and in the press.

Debt of Honour

In the darkness there was light, and in the light there was hope. Stannard could hear the snakes slithering on their bellies all around him and he shivered. He had never liked snakes and these were Indian Cobras. He reached for the shattered torch. It no longer functioned of course, but it offered some small protection if any of the cobras developed evil intentions. God, how long had he been down there, and what was the time?

He pondered on how he came to be in the deep hundred foot pit and swore again out loud. The lure of finding ancient artefacts had been too strong and he'd climbed down, never realising that the rope would fray under his bulky weight and snap, and send him plunging, back-first, one hundred feet into the snake pit. And there were scores of snakes, large, small and giant, slithering crookedly over his boots and his arms.

His back was broken and movement was impossible but he could move his arms at least, if not his legs. 'Get away, you ugly brute!' he roared as a cobra reared up on its coils and hovered by his face. The sound of the torch striking viciously made a dry sucking sound like someone skidding on a squashed peach, and he felt revolted.

'Can you hear me?' he shouted at the top of his lungs. 'I'm stuck down this blasted pit, and can't get out!'

His failing voice faded away into a dim echo, and silence folded back into nothingness. He began to feel panic rising inside as two or three more large shapes swayed stoat-fashion nearby. In desperation he waved the heavy rubber torch and watched in horror as his wrist gave way and his fingers lost their grip, sending the black torch sliding out of reach. Now he had nothing to threaten with and save him from the snakes.

He closed his eyes and waited for death, listening to the slithering and faint flicker of hundreds of forked tongues. He knew the cobras had sensed his new helplessness somehow and were just biding their time to strike again, or wait until he was asleep.

'Help me, for God's sake - please someone help me!' he called out again, wincing at the dry soreness of his burning throat.

He promised himself that if a miracle happened and he was rescued that he'd never go in search of antiquities again. Then the faint scratching sound made him stiffen. It sounded like rats in the clay wall trying to scrabble through making his perilous situation doubly horrible. He couldn't stand rats either, it was a particular phobia of his, and had been all his life.

The scratching sounds intensified and dust fell onto his face from above. He quickly shielded his eyes with his left hand. The scratching stopped after a further heavy dustfall and he peeped through the gaps in his fingers, seeming to see two beady eyes looking down at him. He could imagine the whiskers and yellow fangs...

'I shall go mad,' he whispered in anguish. 'Oh, go away!' he screamed as the looming shape of a huge cobra leered at him in the darkness. He punched the scaly flesh and it drew back sharply.

Perhaps they were like sharks in the ocean, he thought, only attacking dead bodies, but afraid of live men who kicked out and made a noise. He stared up at where the dust had fallen down from and strained to hear the rats.

'Sahib,' called a voice. 'Sahib, can you move? Reach up - I have a rope to pull you up with.'

Relief flooded him like a thousand electric bulbs going on at once and he called out urgently. 'I've broken my back and can't move. And there are lots of snakes down here. For God's sake be careful!'

'I have something for the snakes,' said the voice, letting something furry down. A warm moist nose brushed his mouth and tickled his lips with quivering whiskers and he recoiled. 'It is a mongoose, Sahib,' called the voice reassuringly. 'Do not worry. And I have one for every snake.'

Ten or so more furry forms plopped down all around him and grappled in the darkness as the slithering increased. Something cold crawled over his arm and he grabbed it in his fist and brought it close. A scorpion! He threw it down shaking. A scorpion's sting in that country was deadly poisonous to humans.

'The rope I shall tie around your waist, Sahib,' said the voice in his ear, 'but it may hurt you. Please prepare yourself.'

He blacked out. Coming to in his comfortable hotel room with cooling fans wafting pleasantly over his bare skin, he found to his surprise that he could sit up, and did so. He reached for the silk tasselled bell pull and tugged it hard. Running feet sounded on the terracotta tiles in the corridor and the door opened to reveal a European face.

'Ah, Harding,' he said. 'Can you tell me anything about the man who saved me and brought me here. I'd like to thank him.'

'I am sorry, Commissioner,' said the secretary, 'he left without giving his name.'

'Very well, Harding. But I'm going back to the dig today, do you understand?'

'But sir, is that wise? You've been very ill.'

'Nonsense! Get me up and dressed, and fetch me a wheelchair, Harding.'

The dig was all bustle and filled up with native diggers balancing large baskets full of clay soil on their turbanned heads. The dig constable, Abdul Fakir, approached discreetly. 'Sahib, we have caught a grave robber stealing treasures,' he said in a serious voice.

'Bring him to me.'

'Very well, Sahib, but he is dangerous and has killed a policeman.'

'Has he? Then he shall be dealt with very severely. As you are aware, as the Commissioner for Archaeological Sites I am empowered to impose the death penalty automatically on both white men and black. Where is this man?'

'Here, he is sir,' said Major Harding. 'Caught with gold carvings and other precious items, and killed a Sikh policeman trying to get away.'

The Commissioner sat in the wheelchair and examined the scrawny figure with the single shifting eye and shook his head. 'A case of mistaken identity,' he said firmly. 'Let him go.'

'But sir!'

'I said let him go, Harding. That's an order. Sergeant Afrid - what's the man's name?'

'Hassan Dimpley, Sahib.'

'Well, in case Mr. Dimpley doesn't speak English sergeant, will you ask him what he was doing last Wednesday night?'

There was a whispered conference between the sergeant and the accused man, who gestured and shouted. The police sergeant straightened up. 'He says he was washing the camels of his cousin, sir.'

Stannard nodded and smiled.

'Then please thank Mister Hassan Dimpley for washing the camels of his cousin so well!' he growled with mock severity. 'And give him this wristwatch from me.'

Tea for Two

Donald Strang stared down at the smashed-up car in dismay. His expensive and brand new silver Mercedes lay half-in and half-out of the deep roadside ditch full of icy water, compressed snow clinging to its tyres, and clogging that part of the shattered windscreen that he could see.

He shook his head to clear it. He'd been very lucky indeed to escape unscathed when the vehicle skidded off the road at 70 m.p.h. after colliding head-on with the thick snowdrifts blocking the way ahead, making it impassable.

He shivered in his white tuxedo, black dress trousers, and thin shirt and bow tie. He had no hat or coat, or scarf and gloves. After all, no accident is ever planned for, and sliding off the road at high speed into the ditch like that had been the very last thing he had expected to happen, at three a.m. on his way home from the late-night party.

And now, he was standing alone in the pitch darkness on an isolated country road miles from anywhere, getting soaked through from the freezing rain that was just beginning to fall, and making things infinitely more miserable. There was not even a torch in the glove compartment, or the boot of the car, to light his way and provide some small measure of comfort.

Well, it was no use counting the financial cost - the new silver Mercedes was not yet insured - he had only taken delivery of it the previous afternoon. And, in any case, he had to find some place from where he could ring his wife, so she could come out and collect him. That is, of course, if he could tell her where he was himself. The fields and skeletal trees, and even the animals he could hear slowly moving about behind the hedges cropping the few shoots poking above the blanket of snow, seemed featureless and all the same.

He glanced briefly up at the moonless sky before setting off, looking directly into the driving sheets of steadily falling drizzle, and averted his face. It was a filthy, cold and bitter January night.

Pulling up his jacket's inadequate collar to protect his exposed neck, he blew on his hands to warm them, lengthening his stride as his sopping wet black patent leather shoes crunched and slithered over the snow, stark-white in contrast and blinding to his eyes, treacherous to life and limb and pockmarked by the rain.

There had to be some kind of dwelling soon. Some farm he might come across where he could knock up the occupant, and, after apologising for the lateness of the hour, make that all-important phone call to his wife, so she could speed out and collect him.

Then he could report the Mercedes stolen first thing when he got up and brief his wife on what she should say to alibi him, if there were awkward questions asked despite his official position.

Thinking of this made him glance behind fearfully for he thought he heard the sound of a vehicle approaching, driving slowly and deliberately. The very last thing he wanted at that moment was for a police car to come along and pick him out in its headlights. What would he answer when they asked if the crashed Mercedes they'd just seen back in the ditch was his? And how could he hide the fact that he'd had a lot to drink at the private party with his legal friends, and given by Sir Gerald Battersby, the eminent barrister? The police would have no other choice than to charge him and put him under arrest. It would be highly embarrassing for Sir Gerald and devastating for him. He shuddered at the thought.

But he had imagined the car he thought he'd heard. An echo from some distance away, from one of the busier main roads he supposed; all was still and quiet behind him for as far as he could see with the naked eye. If the police *did* come he would simply throw himself over the hedge that ran parallel to the road he was walking on at that moment. Such a thing was simple enough.

He was in his seventies but still quite agile enough for that, and he'd been very fit when he was younger, having run for Scotland in the Olympic Games on one very proud occasion.

Even so, he hoped he wouldn't have to suffer that particular indignity, and besides, as soon as the police saw the silver car in the ditch and checked on who owned it, they'd go straight round and knock up Edith, who would innocently tell them the truth. That he'd driven to a party of boozy legal friends and he hadn't come home. The thought of the headlines in the more sensational tabloids drove him on, and then his heart gave a lurch. A tiny glimmer of light showed through the trees over to the left, indicating that someone who lived there was still up.

Clambering over a two strand barbed-wire fence and ripping one leg of his dress trousers in the process, he scurried, panting heavily, across the field, and drenched and frozen to the bone, rang the bell in the brightly lit-up porch.

While he waited for someone to come in answer, he examined where he was, just for something to do. A tall pair of black wellingtons had been left untidily on the step together with two mud-stiff brown woollen gloves thrown down any old how - he wondered what the householder would look like.

The door shook and trembled as bolts were drawn back inside and was then pulled open and held wide. Strang stepped back in amazement and surprise. The man framed in the doorway was quite unexpected, given the locality and the lateness of the hour.

He was scruffy and bearded, his face scarred horribly from his eyebrow to his chin, he had only half an ear and wore a black patch over one eye. But that was not what staggered Strang so much. It was the fact that he was wearing a blue and orange printed frock, pendulous ear rings, and pink sparkly high-heeled shoes!

'Good God!' he exclaimed, momentarily forgetting his errand and his extreme need for warmth and shelter.

'What is it?'

'I need to make an urgent telephone call. I know it's very late and all that, but would you mind awfully. I'm very cold...'

'Sure. Come in. I am a true believer and welcome lost travellers as in days of old. There's hot coffee on the stove, or I've got tea if you'd prefer. Don't mind the cats. I'm afraid they've had the run of the place and think the furniture is their own.'

'Thank you. Have you a telephone?'

'A telephone? Why, no. I had it taken out when my father died.'

Strang sat down gingerly and ill at ease in a high-backed armchair. All the furniture in the room where he was, including the curtains and the thick-pile carpet were extremely expensive-looking and of the highest quality. He was appalled to see at least twenty cats adorning the sideboard and the dining table and even several more gathered around the blazing fire in the hearth.

'What did your father do? It's a very fine house,' he ventured, when his weirdly-dressed host brought him the tea he'd asked for in a priceless Royal Doulton cup, emblazoned with a heraldic crest with a latin inscription.

'Oh, this and that, you know,' replied the man in the frock and eye patch, matter-of-factly. 'I say, do you like these shoes? I got them from Harrods in the sale, along with that hat over there.'

Donald Strang shifted uneasily and looked over at the hat - a strange affair with lime green ostrich feathers and a pink veil - lying amongst some sedate Siamese cats and a fat ginger moggy which was actually reclining upon it and crushing it out of shape with its enormous bulk. But his spirit failed him at the last moment, and he found he was quite incapable of commenting, even at the risk of appearing rude.

'You don't like hats very much then?' asked the other man smiling broadly.

'No, not much,' admitted the guest, fidgeting against a compelling and urgent need to giggle nervously, which was all but impossible to shake off. 'Thank you for the hot tea,' he said miserably. 'Shall I take the empty cup out into the kitchen?'

'If you like, dear,' said the man with the patch.

Out in the sumptuously-decorated kitchen full of the latest labour-saving devices, its walls lined neatly with burnished copper saucepans and gleaming stainless-steel utensils and sieves, he nodded approvingly. At least everything was clean!

Then he saw the oil painting and knew it was an original. The thing took his breath away completely, for he knew a thing or two about art and was certain that it was a Constable of some quality.

'A very nice painting in the kitchen,' commented Strang, returning to the front room again. 'I say, it is very good of you to let me stay the night like this.'

The man in the frock smiled and absently fondled a blue-cream Burmese which had just plonked itself on his lap and was in the process of kneading his stockings with its claws. 'You can have the painting if you like. What do you do for a living then, my dear? Not a plumber are you, only I need a plumber because the bath upstairs leaks from time to time.'

'I'm a crown court judge,' admitted Donald Strang self-consciously.

'A judge!' echoed the man in the eye patch cheerfully. 'Well, there's a thing, puss, isn't it now?'

The Burmese cat looked up into the scarred and battered face adoringly and Strang looked away, wondering how on earth he could pass the many hours until it would be light enough for him to make his escape from such odd company. He had never particularly liked cats and his strange companion's choice of clothes embarrassed him immensely.

'What's your name, dear?'

'Donald Strang.'

'Are your clothes wet, Mister Strang? You can wear one of my frocks if you like till your own things dry out. There's hundreds in the wardrobe up in my bedroom.'

'Er... no thank you,' said Strang, swallowing hard. 'Could I possibly use your lavatory though, to freshen up?'

'Yes, use the one upstairs.'

At the top of the stairs the unwilling guest paused. So many cream-painted and closed doors confronted him. He saw they all had tastefully-made brass nameplates such as 'Phil's Room', 'Margaret's Hovel' and 'Mother's Bedroom'. Finding the one marked 'Lavvy', he went straight in and shut the door behind him.

The place where he was at that moment reeked of opulence in

every pore. The wall mirror was edged with gold and pale blue lapis lazuli and the taps on the sink were solid silver, whilst the toilet pedestal was blue and white Delft topped by a luxurious, and as he soon found out, divinely comfortable ermine fur-covered seat.

Smiling after his brief visit Donald Strang wiped his hands on a monogrammed ivory cotton towel and helped himself to a dash of cologne from a large bottle standing on a shelf along with five ornate toothbrushes on a platinum rack above the wash basin. Then he returned downstairs to the front room where his host began talking in a lively way once again.

'This house has seven hundred acres of parkland out there with herds of red deer and rare breed cattle, you know.'

'I think that you are very fortunate, sir, to live in such wonderfully peaceful and idyllic surroundings,' said Donald.

'You'd think so, wouldn't you dear, but you know material possessions can be such an anchor to one's spirit. Did you like that big Ming vase you saw at the top of the stairs, by the way? It came all the way from China.'

'It's quite magnificent. But I had no idea that it was a genuine one from the Ming Dynasty.'

'Oh yes, it's the real thing. You can have *that* too if you like, along with that picture out in the kitchen that you commented on earlier. Material things mean nothing to me you know, dear. All I wish is for my sinful life to be over and to meet the Lord.'

'You shouldn't talk like that,' said Donald Strang, now deep in thought. 'You look very healthy indeed, as a matter of fact, if you don't mind my saying so.'

'Do I, dear? Well, that's very nice of you I must say.'

'That little green statue of the dragon above the mantelpiece in front of us, is that from China too?'

'Why yes, it is. Made of jade that one, and worth a fortune I should think. But I have never liked it, so you have it, dear, go on, take it down and put it by your chair so you can take it when you go. Another cup of tea, dear?'

'Yes, the last one was very nice and in such a pretty cup too. But, I couldn't possibly take advantage of your generosity regarding the things you have mentioned. It is rather exquisite though.'

'Nonsense. I'll have the picture, the vase and the dragon wrapped in newspaper and placed in a nice big cardboard box so you can take it with you. And as you like the cup you had your tea in so much I'll give you the whole teaset if you like. There's 60 pieces in all. My late father brought it back from Russia just after the revolution.'

Three months later, Donald Strang was due to sit on the bench at Maidenhead Crown Court trying a difficult case. As he waited in his robing room, resplendent in scarlet gown, white tabs, black silk cassock and full-bodied grey-wool wig, he heard the usher announce him.

'His honour Judge Strang will be presiding in this case. All persons having business in the case of Crown versus Patterson-Hope shall draw near and give their attendance, giving their evidence impartially and in good faith, and without fear or favour. Please be upstanding for his honour the Judge.'

Donald slipped silently through the private entrance to the left of the Lion and Unicorn crest below the royal crown and took his place on the high bench, summoning his fiercest professional glare and directing it at the dock where the defendant stood.

In his opinion and experience he tended to err on the side of caution in criminal cases that he tried.

Nine times out of ten the wretches were all as guilty as sin with only extremely clever counsel convincing the jury of their innocence, by trickery, at the last moment. He was determined today to find the felon guilty, whoever he was, and brook no nonsense from defending counsel, who happened to be his old arch-enemy Grabwell Trout, who had bullied him unmercifully at his minor public school.

The defendant sat down in the dock as Donald began writing laboriously in his thick ledger up on the bench and he tersely ordered the clerk to state the evidence in the case.

'David Patterson-Hope, you are charged with fifteen counts of burglary and going equipped to commit a felony, how do you plead?'

'Stand up, man!' cried out his honour Judge Strang at the prisoner who remained stubbornly sitting down and obscured by the high Victorian cast-iron railings.

'I plead guilty as charged, sir,' said the man, and Donald sighed in irritation. What he wanted was a firm 'Not Guilty' plea so he could sabotage the defence by summing up in favour of the crown, and strongly influencing the jury. This was no good at all and spoiled everything.

Then he gaped in genuine astonishment, for the prisoner who smiled crookedly back at him from the dock wore an eye patch on his scarred face, and dangly ear rings, and a frock with a tilted orange-feathered hat.

'You!' he whispered in dismay.

'Yes dear, it's me,' taunted the defendant, smiling broadly.

The judge wiped his brow with a handkerchief and ordered the evidence read out in full. His mind seethed with conflicting emotions of personal guilt and violent anger.

'There are many individual charges against this prisoner who has been a professional burglar all his life,' intoned the police inspector of detectives to the court as the judge sat up on his bench watching malevolently.

'The fact is, your honour, many of the thefts do not really matter and pale into insignificance in the light of one particularly disgraceful incident, whereby this man, Patterson-Hope, broke into the holiday home of our most gracious sovereign the Queen, and unlawfully removed several valuable items which have never been found. Under questioning at the police station he has not said a single word as to their whereabouts and Her Majesty is anxious to get her things back, particularly a very attractive and rare Royal Doulton tea set given her by her grandmother, and which once belonged to Queen Victoria.   In addition   to the said item there is a Constable masterpiece worth over ten million pounds, a Ming vase worth nearly the same, and a very valuable jade dragon, the property of the Red Chinese government and on loan to her Majesty. This loss has almost caused an international political incident, which only the Prime Minister himself could calm in time before China recalled her ambassador and declared war on this country. I strongly urge that this man be given the longest sentence it is possible to give, and that he be sentenced separately for each burglary, instead of all the offences being taken together, concurrently, as normal. I say this because this person was a very plausible man who often obtained entry to even the most respectable of households by the device of dressing up in frocks and ear rings, making illegal entry to ladies' dressing rooms and boudoirs far more easily than would have been the case in normal male attire.'

In his summing up which was extremely brief and to the point, his honour Judge Strang, was particularly anxious, he said, to make any punishment he inflicted, fit the crime.

'This is indeed a very serious crime, committed as it was against the august person of her Majesty the Queen herself. I understand that the convicted man made a dreadful mess at the scene, bringing back stray cats from all over the neighbourhood and that the dry-cleaning bills and fumigation costs are enormous. Notwithstanding this feature which is disgraceful enough, he has stubbornly refused, even under the most intense pressure, to tell the police where the stolen articles are to be found, and I shall bear this in mind when coming to sentencing. What the prisoner in the meantime might think about as pressing directly down upon him is firstly that any court over which I have jurisdiction shall not assist any criminal who might be counting on living on ill-gotten gains after his release and hoping for a light sentence in order to do this. Let me disabuse you of that right away, for I am not given to dishing out light sentences. That having been said, there is another point the accused might do well to ponder in addition. Were it not for the passage of several enlightened centuries, he might in another place, and at a different time, not merely be facing an inevitable custodial sentence, for what he has done to the monarch, but hanging, drawing and quartering in a public place, after first having had to suffer the indignity of having his tongue and toenails pulled out by the roots with long pliers first.'

The prisoner in his eye patch and frock smiled knowingly and said just audibly enough, 'I made you tea, my dear.' Donald Strang rushed on with what he had to say.

'Stand up for sentencing, Patterson-Hope,' he thundered, 'and take that damned silly smile off your lips. Burglary, for anybody, is a very serious matter and is a crime all too common in these days. David Patterson-Hope, you are a menace to civilised society. I propose therefore to make an example of you because you are brazen and clearly regard yourself as a burglar by trade, who I am told has been sent to prison for half of his adult life. Prison then, has proved ineffectual in your case, and yet the gravity of your crimes demands this. You go to prison, but I do not intend fixing the minimum time you are to serve, but rather to leave that open-ended - making it a condition of imprisonment that you are confined only, and until, the formerly mentioned valuable lost property of the Queen is returned in full. Therefore, you will stay in prison until such time as this is acheived. Take him down, constable.'

At home that evening, the judge made two separate phone calls spaced twenty-four hours apart. 'Hello, Daphne, you know that Chinese vase I gave you? And the other things? Well, I want you to take them to the town pawnbrokers and pledge them all for fifty pounds. Do you understand? Do it first thing tomorrow morning please, and don't forget, because it is important. Yes, yes, I know they are worth far more than that, but that is what I want you to do. Daphne, *you will obey me* in this, and don't tell your mother under any circumstances!'

The second call was made the next evening to Scotland Yard, using a disguised voice: 'Hello, Scotland Yard? You may be interested to know that the items stolen recently from the Queen's holiday cottage in Windsor have turned up undamaged in the pawn shop in Maidenhead. What? Who am I? Oh, just a humble student of human nature, that's all.'

Donald Strang replaced the receiver with a satisfied smile. He had almost discharged his debt of honour. The only thing left to do now was to put the £50 his daughter Daphne had given him into an envelope with a brief note, and address it to Wormwood Scrubs Prison.

'Hello, my dear,' he wrote, 'please find enclosed enough to buy a nice new frock and some ear rings, to celebrate your release.'

Charlatan's Reward

Although the Bishop of Aldington was officially employed by the Church of England as an Exorcist, he did not himself strictly believe in the supernatural. Neither was he particularly religious. But the massaging of his ego that came from the dual prestige and kudos he received both from being a high-ranking clergyman with a large and prosperous congregation, and the aura of mystique endowed by his official post, fully made up for this deficiency.

The Bishop found soon after being appointed by the Archbishop of Canterbury, that in no time he could talk the most utter nonsense at great length about poltergeists quoting from non-existent past cases, and he enjoyed being the sole authority, to a gullible audience on the Transpersonal Progression of Demons, an imaginary state of his own devising, about which he had already written sixteen books.

Christmas Eve 1999 found the Bishop in his study reading his Christmas cards, always a lengthy task. He received many from all over the world from admiring cranks, these often contained heart-felt pleas concerning resident ghosts that simply must be got rid of as they were driving the family concerned mad, and scaring the horses. Could the Bishop of Aldington, by using his famous skills, not pop over for a day or two, for a fat fee, and banish the ghost?

The Bishop was in high good humour as he sat at his desk by the window reading the card in his hand. It really was an example of an idiot's paradise. He roared with laughter and laid it down, looking out with an amused face at the silently falling snow covering the immaculate lawns and tidy beds of his palace garden, near Dorking. Sniggering again, he took the card up and re-read it.

'Dear Bishop of Aldington, Reverend Sir,' it began. 'We are plagued here by the spirit of a long-dead surgeon who once owned the hall. All the time there is the unearthly sound of chains rattling, objects dropped heavily on the floorboards above, and eerie laughter after

16

midnight.   Please, for the love of God, journey down here to Wiltshire, and rid us of this pestilence. Money no object. Please take the next train. Sir Ivor Canby. F.R.C.S.'

The Bishop smiled broadly and tapped the Christmas card containing the message. There was a telephone number which he immediately dialled. Sir Ivor, the owner of Oak Hall, snatched up the receiver the other end and confirmed the parlous state of affairs.

'Lord Bishop,' he beseeched, 'I am in desperate straits. You must come at once. Last night really took the biscuit as far as I am concerned. This apparition took the form of a monstrous black hound that leapt on the cook in her room in the attic, and tried to er... have its way with her carnally. The female staff have left en masse after hearing of it and refuse to return to my employment, for love nor money.'

'My fee would be large for such a difficult case,' interjected the Bishop quickly. 'You realise that?'

'My dear fellow, I have tried everything before coming to you, believe me. We have hung garlic in the kitchen, sprinkled salt on the stairs, and left out poisoned bones and pies in an animal dish, but it is still here. I would pay a million pounds to rid my house of this fiend from hell!'

'A million pounds!' exclaimed the Bishop.   'That will not be necessary I assure you.'   Then, becoming bolder, he added: 'Of course, I was thinking a hundred thousand pounds might be appropriate, seeing as this thing, this incontinent spectral dog, is causing you so much trouble. How does that sound to you?'

'I will give you more, much more, if only you will come,' came the voice from the receiver, sounding heart-rending in the extreme.

'Right then, I will take your advice in the card, and catch the next train down,' said the Bishop. 'But do be aware that it is Christmas Eve, and I am putting myself out. I would expect a hot meal and a liqueur on arrival at the very least.'

When he had rung off, the Bishop of Aldington rubbed his hands with pleasure. A hundred thousand pounds for just one night's work! It was unbelieveable what these deluded fools would pay to get rid of, what was as often as not, only something from their imaginations, playing on their own nervous fears. Sometimes he even wished there were such things as ghosts, if only to to still the voice of his conscience, but this last had long ago been silenced and sold off to quite another kind of supernatural entity.

The Bishop packed a small case and rang a cab to take him to the railway station, and was soon hurtling through the Hampshire countryside en-route for deepest Wiltshire.

Oak Hall was situated on the edge of a mist-draped stretch of moorland, twelve miles outside of Melkesham, and the Bishop had little trouble getting a taxi driver to find it. On being dropped off the Bishop asked the fare.

'Now let me see, sir. That will be seven pounds exactly,' said the driver brightly. 'Ah, a tenner. Keep the change shall I, sir, as it's Christmas Eve?'

'Certainly not!' snapped the Bishop crossly. 'I will take my correct change of three pounds, thank you, and not a penny less.'

He stood in the drive at the bottom of the steps leading up to the ivy-covered porch over the massive studded door, and smiled to himself. The place certainly looked the part of a haunted house with its perpendicular architecture, arched windows, and dark unlit wings. He climbed the steps and put down his case, pulling the bell with a firm jerk. A long drawn-out pealing echoed through the silent building, shortly afterwards the porch light was snapped on, and a slithering inside accompanied by heavy breathing marked the approach of somebody in carpet slippers coming to the summons. Many bolts were pulled back one by one, and the door creaked inwards. A jolly-looking man with a pink face and cotton wool flyaway hair stood there.

'Bishop Aldington, is that you?' he cried gaily. 'Come in, my dear sir. You have no idea how relieved I am to see you. Let me take your things.'

When he had rebolted the front door, The pink-faced man turned to him with serious eyes. 'A room has been prepared for you with a blazing log fire, it will take the chill out of your bones on such a cold night. I am Sir Ivor Canby, by the way. The one who wrote to you. It has got worse incidentally, since I spoke to you on the phone.'

'What has?'

'Why, the ghost. It has taken to picking on innocent domestic pets now. The cat died of fright just before you arrived, and the parrot. My goodness the parrot. Do you know what it has done to the poor parrot?'

'I obviously have no idea,' said the Bishop sarcastically. He was far more interested in a liqueur and a hot meal than talk about dead cats and stupid parrots.

'The poor parrot,' repeated the owner, shaking his head sorrowfully. 'The poor parrot.'

'What is up with the blessed bird then?' demanded the Bishop irritably. 'I suppose it has run off in terror from this ghostly apparition.'

Sir Ivor Canby looked startled.

'Not exactly no. I mean it would have done if it could have, its wings being clipped and all. But the fiend has snapped its feet off. Both of them, one after the other. Just like that, with the most inhuman and unimaginable force! I found them chucked under the sideboard in the front room.'

'You had better take me to my room at once, Sir Ivor', said the Bishop tensely. 'I have yet to eat, you know. Where is the room by the way, on the ground floor?'

'No. Upstairs in the East Wing, next to mine. But Bishop, I entreat you. For the sake of my sanity deal with this horrible presence before you even think of dining. We cannot waste another second, and I fully believe both of our lives are in the gravest danger all the time this evil thing is free to work its horrors. I will of course pay you extra. Shall we say another hundred thousand on top of what we already agreed, if you forsake your comfort now, and set about your work? Only I am convinced that this thing intends to kill me. You see, this dead surgeon used to own the Hall, and he's jealous of me buying it.'

'Very well,' said the Bishop briskly. 'Fetch me up that case and I will lay out my things at once.'

Frowning with ill-humour, he laid out his exorcist kit with very bad grace, on the stone-flagged kitchen floor. 'Let me see what we have. Oh yes, the book on Alchemy and spells, phial of Holy Water and a silver and wood crucifix. The chalk for the circle, and the chalcedony and wax incense. Oh, and we mustn't forget the most important thing of all. A piece of the true cross smuggled over to France by a Roman Centurion after Our Lord's agonising death at Calvary. Have you any candles, by the way? In my haste to come to your aid I seem to have left mine at home. If you have black ones they are of course best, but any colour will do, even plain white.'

'Candles sir? Why yes, I use them all the time to save electricity. I shall fetch you some immediately. How many do you need? Will fourteen be enough? Only it may be a longer night than you bargained for.'

'Nonsense. I am a world authority on these things. Why, Dennis Wheatley even based his books on me! You just cut along now about your business, and leave me to mine. When you have fetched the candles you can toddle off to bed if you like, you'll only be in the way here. I must have space to work if I am to defeat the cunning of this spectral dog.'

Sir Ivor Canby regarded him thoughtfully.

'If you are sure you'll be alright then,' he said, his voice trailing off. 'To tell the truth, I have had more than enough of this dead surgeon, I don't mind saying. What will happen to him then?'

The Bishop tapped the side of his nose and winked. 'Let us not air the Devil's laundry, my friend,' he said mysteriously. 'Now get along and fetch those candles, you silly little man. The clock has struck eleven thirty and Satan will no doubt shortly send his minions out in their legions, to torment us and despoil our sleep.'

A few minutes later Sir Ivor Canby brought two handfuls of pale yellow candles and plonked them down on the dresser, watching the Bishop's back bowed in prayer.

'Goodnight then, sir,' he said softly.

The Bishop rose and stared at him fiercely. 'I am communing with the spirits!' he cried. 'How dare you presume to interrupt.'

'I am so sorry sir,' said Sir Ivor, going out, and shutting the kitchen door with downcast eyes.

The Bishop heard his soft footfalls going up the stairs and receding into the depths of the quiet old house.

The Bishop helped himself to a cigar from a box on the window sill as silence fell like a damp blanket, the night wind blew eerily through the trees in the grounds outside and against the eaves of the Medieval half-timbered Hall. It would be so easy to allow himself to become affected by such things, but he was made of sterner stuff than that. He merely chuckled out loud and sat at the kitchen table thinking how long he could decently hang things out before calling the old man down and announcing that his home had been successfully exorcised, and the ghost banished forever.

Becoming bored, he searched the cupboards where he was for alcohol. The cupboards remained stubbornly bare. 'The old boy must keep a bottle somewhere,' he said out loud. 'It must be in the library.'

He went there and scanned the great bookcases filled with priceless tooled leather volumes. None there either. Or in the drawing room, or any of the downstairs rooms. In desperation, he returned to the kitchen and took down the half-empty bottle of cooking sherry he had noticed earlier, perched above the two Agas. 'He'll damned well pay for this outrage,' muttered his lordship, having to face a long night all alone in a strange old house that made creaking noises all the time as the timbers settled, and with fingers of ivy scratching against the window panes, jarring him out of his wits. He swigged morosely, emptying the contents and throwing the bottle into the corner, where it rolled insolently, before coming to a stop under a chair. Eventually he fell asleep.

He was awoken by someone rudely pulling and yanking at his shoulder, and the sun streaming down onto his face from the unshuttered window. A family stood looking down at him angrily. Mother, an American father, and seven children in the very latest thing in designer wear for tots and teenagers.

'Say, what are you doing in our kitchen?' asked the man.

'And what are you doing with my bottle of cooking wine; we are Quakers!' stormed the woman, snatching it up from beneath the chair, and glaring at him darkly.

The Bishop rubbed at his eyes and smoothed his rumpled cassock down in outraged embarrassment.

'Where is Sir Ivor Canby?' he thundered. 'Fetch him here at once. I want my money.'

'What money?' asked the American father.

'The two hundred thousand pounds he owes me for getting rid of the ghost and making his house safe and peaceful again. What do you think I was referring to, you idiot?'

The American smiled and exchanged glances with his wife. 'Ah, so you met up with Sir Ivor Canby, I guess. The old surgeon. That's good. We rather like him. Though the estate agent told my wife when we first moved here that the old boy might be troublesome, as when he was alive he was so fond of playing practical jokes. Say mister, you look pale. Don't you believe that a ghost can play jokes?'

Loose Talk

Applause echoed around the winning enclosure as Stephen Foster walked up to the baize-draped trophy stand and accepted his prize for the Mallard Stakes. Holding the boxed silver cuff links aloft he smiled as the press cameras clicked, and stepped down to be immediately pinholed by a reporter.

'How does it feel to ride your 300th. winner, Mister Foster?'

'Strangely flat,' replied the champion jockey with a boyish grin. 'The Mallard Stakes was just another race. Excuse me, my fiancée's waiting for me in the restaurant and she's come all the way from Yorkshire.'

Over coffee the jockey began to discuss the day's rides. 'I'm on Black Stranger, trained by Arthur Smith, in the next,' he said. 'And then I'm riding two more of his. Cloak of Erin, and Wildaway.'

'So, you might even add a couple of other winners to your 300 before the day is out,' said his fiancée Virginia, admiringly.

Stephen Foster smiled and looked down into his coffee cup wearing a rueful expression. 'No, none of them has any chance at all,' he announced quietly. 'Black Stranger, in particular, is the worst jumper in the land. I wouldn't accept him for dog's meat.'

A man in a check suit with a yellow rose in the lapel rose abruptly and left the dining room, unseen by the jockey and his attractive female companion.

The day worked out just as the jockey had said it would. His three rides came nowhere and his score in the current championship remained stuck on 300.

'Never mind,' said his fiancée. 'Not many jockeys are good enough to clock up so many winners in a single season, and there's still 6 weeks left yet, with your nearest rival fifty or more behind. The Jockey's Championship is certain to be yours for the fifth time, in a row.' She looked at him with shining eyes. 'I want you to know that

I am really proud of you, Steve. The main thing is, you've done it all honestly, and without 'pulling a horse', or falling into the clutches of evil bookmakers.'

The jockey laid an affectionate hand on her sleeve. 'Thanks for saying that, Ginny,' said Stephen Foster gratefully. 'Come on, let's take you home in my new Ferrari. It does 180 m.p.h. in third gear and it's a hell of a lot faster than Arthur Smith's Black Stranger, I can tell you!' They both laughed, and she slipped her arm through her strong boyfriend's, as they walked towards the car park.

The telephone rang at Stephen Foster's Suffolk Georgian farmhouse. 'Yes, who is it?' he asked, cradling the receiver under his chin as he turned the pages of his racing newspaper, studying the next day's form.

'Have you seen the front page of the *News of the World*?' demanded a voice the other end, which belonged to the trainer, Arthur Smith.

'Well no,' said Stephen Foster, mystified. 'Have we bombed Iraq again?'

'No,' thundered Arthur Smith, a blunt Lancastrian. 'There's a bad picture of you, and a quote that makes my blood boil. I'll read it to you. 'I WOULDN'T HAVE THIS NAG FOR DOG'S MEAT'. Does it ring a bell, at all? I tell you, Foster, you'll get no more rides from me, or any of my friends either, and that includes Lady Cynthia Clark.'

Stephen Foster blushed and stammered. Lady Cynthia Clark had been the means of providing him with most of his winners the past four seasons. Without her patronage he could count on only single figures from chance rides, and he'd miss the lucrative retainer that she always paid him. Besides, If she dumped him, all his best rides would go to Johnny Legg, his nearest rival.

'Mister Smith,' he answered, thinking quickly. 'I can explain.' But a continuous buzzing told him that the irate trainer had rung off in high dudgeon.

'I'll definitely keep my mouth shut in future,' he vowed, boiling up the kettle for his bedtime cocoa.

The meeting at Fontwell dawned foggy and drizzling, adding to his woes. He was riding a horse called Brandyline Bear in the first - a stocky bay with a bloodline going back to Arkle and Golden Miller.

Mounting up, he spotted a crowd of racing reporters who began to call out loaded remarks and bombarded him with questions about the controversial article in the Sunday tabloid. 'I'll turn the tables now,' he thought to himself.

Beckoning to one who wore a padded wax jacket and jeans, he leaned down from the saddle conspiratorially. 'I may as well tell you this,' he said. 'This horse I'm on is extremely fit and will win by at least 20 lengths. But don't tell anyone else. We're trying to keep it a secret. It's 12/1 at the moment and you'll definitely clean up.'

The man grinned broadly. 'Thanks Steve. And, don't worry, I won't breathe a word.'

Stephen Foster smiled inwardly. The bay was a good horse alright, and under normal conditions would fly home to win, but it had rained heavily the past three days and it hated soft going. He might make fourth or even third, but he couldn't win. The owners and the trainer knew that too and were running him to keep his fitness up.

But, unfortunately, Brandyline Bear found inner reserves of speed and stamina, and won clearly when several more fancied horses fell at the last. Stephen Foster had done the press, who'd damaged his career so much, an inadvertent favour.

'Thanks, Steve,' chorused the reporters, waving wads of cash. 'We'll give you a good write-up this time, don't worry!'

Later that evening the phone rang.

'Yes, this is Stephen Foster, who is that?'

'The Jockey Club,' said a well-bred voice. 'Mister Foster, I wonder if you can comment on some disturbing information we've received about your ride on Brandyline Bear, at Fontwell, today. A journalist from the Sporting Year has stated that you told him the horse was doped to win.'

The Sitting Tenant

The well-heeled couple from Hampstead drove in through the stone pillars and up the long drive, admiring the acres of lush green parkland, neat clumps of ancient elm trees and the Grade One weathered limestone mansion that lay ahead of them under the bright sunshine.

Pulling the midnight-blue and cream Rolls Royce to a stop in front of the entrance with its imposing Corinthian pillars they got out, straightening their crumpled designer clothes, gazing in awe at the long windows adorning the massive front which towered above them for a further three storeys.

'Look Jim,' said the woman in an undertone, 'sixteen chimneys on the roof.'

Her husband, James Stillway, said nothing, and nudged her as a young butler in formal black morning coat and stiff white shirt front and bow tie emerged briskly from the entrance and greeted them with a smile of welcome.

'Mr and Mrs Stillway?' he said with a slight bow. 'The master said you would be arriving in your car at about this time. Welcome to Crumley Hall.'

'Thank you,' they replied and followed him meekly up the broad steps and into the darkened hall, paved with diagonal lines of miniature black and white enamelled tiles and lined with valuable oil paintings of the owner's past ancestors.

'I like that porcelain cherub on the stand,' whispered Doris Stillway to her husband approvingly as the butler, whom they learned was called Charles, showed them into the most tastefully and expensively furnished room they had ever seen.

'If you'll wait here sir, I'll inform the master that you have arrived,' said the butler. 'He is in the conservatory snipping some orchids for the table.'

'Orchids eh?' said James Stillway in an impressed voice, when they were alone. 'Blimey Dolly, these nobs certainly know how to live in style and comfort, don't they? Eh? Look at that desk, it's French, early sixteenth century and Louis the eleventh. It's worth a bomb. Here, maybe we can negotiate for the furniture and all the fittings at a knock-down price, at the same time!'

They both laughed at the joke as Doris fingered the rich brocades and velvets. Then she gave a little cry of pleasure as her eyes alighted on a wall-hanging depicting hounds and deer, and a royal hunt in a thick forest.

'What does this bloke call himself?' he said out loud. 'Lord summink or other, wasn't it? I'm blessed if I can remember.'

'Not *Lord*, Jimmy,' said Doris severely, glancing down at the visiting card she had just taken out of her handbag. 'The Duke of Avonmouth and March.'

The door swung open silently and another young man stood there with a light brown moustache and rich auburn curly hair.

He was wearing a pink wide-brimmed fedora hat, which he removed, a flowered kaftan and bell-bottomed jeans, while his wrists and neck were covered in tattoos of exotic green snakes and red full-plumaged birds of Paradise. 'Hello,' he said quietly. 'I am Geoffrey March.'

'Pleased to meet you,' said the London antique dealer, and his wife Doris gave an awkward curtsy.

'Please do sit down,' said the young man, removing the soft kid leather gardening gloves he was wearing and indicating a six-legged chaise longue in studded regency stripe satin of green and white. He himself remained standing, leaning with his back against a gold-filigree rimmed oval table that Jimmy Stillway estimated was worth more than his Rolls Royce outside.

'Well now,' said the young man, lighting up a Dunhill filter-tipped cigarette from a platinum and onyx table lighter, and inhaling smoothly. 'As I told you over the telephone, the asking price I had in mind for the house and its contents is in the region of three million.'

Stillway's heart gave a lurch. He had no idea that the quote the man had given him included all of the fine furniture, silver and paintings he had seen so far and lord knew what was in the twelve bedrooms upstairs. The guy must be a mug, he thought, and decided to put this casual assessment to the test.

'Three million is a bit steep,' he said with great earnestness. 'I mean, I know that's what you said to me, and I know after hearing the details of the acreage and estate buildings with the lakes, I agreed in principle. But after actually coming to look for myself I think it's a bit more than I am prepared to pay, your Grace.'

He spread his hands and shrugged as he composed his thick features into an ironic smile which he beamed towards his host. 'Look, Doris is an expert on late medieval tapestries for instance and she sussed out straight away that the one you've got here covering the extent of that wall is a forgery. A clever forgery I grant you, but still a forgery all the same.'

The young man's face darkened in confusion.

'That comes as a bit of a surprise,' he said uncertainly. 'About seven years ago, my father the late Earl, had the tapestry you mention valued at Sothebys just before he died for insurance purposes, and they stated quite categorically that it was worth a hundred and fifty thousand pounds. They also said, by the way, that it was made in Charles the First's time and is the finest example of its kind still in existence.'

'Sothebys,' said James Stillway mockingly. 'These firms are all rogues your Grace, with a vested interest in giving inflated values. That is until you want to sell them something. You'll soon see the price dropping like a stone then, I promise you.'

'Really?' said his host, looking worried. 'Before you spoke to me I had thought that Sothebys had an impeccable reputation. But I will bow to your better judgement as I know nothing about these things, and you appear to be very knowledgeable.'

'James was the head buyer for a large antique importing concern,' said Doris proudly, neglecting to mention that the firm was his own, was run from two phone boxes in a Battersea street, and boasted only an old van without road tax to carry things, at the time. Since then, of course, through a mixture of chicanery, outright dishonesty and bluff, he had made a packet out of house sales, railroading wealthy pensioners who had no idea of what they were parting with, into selling things for a fraction of their worth. That is why they had a large house in Hampstead, a villa on the Algarve, a motorized deep sea-going yacht anchored at Cannes, and were hoping to buy Crumley Hall now.

The young man in the kaftan and jeans shifted and put out his cigarette. 'What price would you consider appropriate then, Mister Stillway?' he asked, turning round with an expression of innocence like a deer that temporarily made the couple feel guilty, but not for long.

Licking his lips, Stillway made a rapid calculation and then smiled like a triumphant snake at the other man. 'A million and a half is my limit,' he said.

As the young man's face fell he quickly qualified what he'd just said: 'Look at the outside of the building. It's badly in need of rendering and that doesn't come cheap. And you've got ivy growing out of the chimneys and over the porch. Some people might consider that looks charming and adds character to a place like this, but I don't. I'd want to rip it down. Not only that, but look at what's cluttering up the inside. No one wants this old-fashioned type of furniture any more, do they? A million and a half your Grace. Take it or leave it. That's my final offer. Ennit, Doris?'

'Yes, it is,' muttered Doris in her flat cockney, her eyes downcast.

'You won't get a better price. Not quickly,' added James Stillway. 'And you did want to sell quickly, didn't you, your lordship?'

'Yes, I did. You see, with my father dying so recently, this house is full of memories which I find disturbing. His spirit is all around and I could never sleep soundly now. Money is not my main concern at the moment. I haven't been in the best of health and therefore my state of mind is of far more importance to me. I get my nervy disposition from my mother's side, you know. All right Stillway, I'll accept. Write me out your cheque and you can move in now if you want.'

'I think you have made exactly the right decision, your Grace,' said James Stillway, fumbling for a pen and his cheque book. 'There we are sir. Your cheque with lots of noughts, and of course the important first part.'

They both laughed. The young man scrutinised the cheque and placed it securely under the base of a jade statue of a Spartan warrior holding a raised javelin on a prancing horse. He held his hand out and James Stillway clasped it briefly.

'Of course, you'll have to give me a few days in which to move out,' he said. 'But I won't need long. I like to travel light. I am an artist who paints watercolours you see, and I am going to live abroad.'

'Whereabouts abroad?' asked Doris.

'The Italian mainland. Well goodbye, Mr and Mrs Stillway, Charles my butler will show you out. I have a slight headache coming on and I'd like to lie down.'

'Here, hang on a minute,' said James Stillway after a furious whispered conversation with Doris. 'What's to prevent you from selling this house again the moment our backs are turned and cashing our cheque? Be a good racket, wouldn't it, selling a place like this five or six times in as many days? Or even one day. I mean, let's face it chum, you were very precise about the time of us coming here weren't you? And a flash Japanese car passed us coming out as we drove in, when we arrived. I'd rather we stayed, if you don't mind, to see that there's no hankey pankey, so to speak.'

The young man fiddled with the end of his moustache and nodded. 'Of course you must stay,' he said picking up the cheque. 'Please tell Charles and he'll make you up a bedroom in the east wing. And as regards your worry about this all being above board, I'll ring my solicitor now. What's the time please?'

'It's half past two,' said Doris.

'Right I'll ring up the senior partner at Croxley's now.' He went over to the phone by the window and picked up the receiver, dialling a number from memory.

'Hello, is that David? Look David, can you motor round here to Crumley Hall straight away. Only I've found a buyer at last. You do have the deeds at your place don't you? Oh, you do? Good. I'll see you about three then. Regards to Cynthia. 'Bye for now...'

He replaced the receiver in its cradle and smiled diffidently. 'My solicitor will be here at three and he'll draw up the contract. How does that suit you, Mister Stillway?'

The young man departed after six days, the Stillways' cheque having been satisfactorily cleared by the local branch of the HSBC bank, and cashed.

James and Doris Stillway, the brash new owners of Crumley Hall waved him away along with his butler Charles in the battered Fiat that he owned.

In the afternoon a car came up the drive - a gleaming Ferrari Fuego with silver bumpers and chromium spoked wheels.

Stillway estimated that there must be at least half a million pounds worth of sports car crunching to a halt on the gravel drive in the bright sunshine in front of him as he came down the steps smirking.

'The house has been sold,' he said baldly, 'so you can sling your hook, old man.'

The driver's door opened and an elegant Gucci foot emerged, followed by a pair of fawn-coloured cord trousers, and a red and black check open-neck shirt with short sleeves accompanied by a tanned forearm from which the brilliant flash of the sun reflected off the solid gold bracelet of a watch.

'What on earth do you mean?' said the sandy-haired stranger, a well-known face from the T.V., removing a pair of dark glasses from his eyes and looking murderous.

'I told you, I have bought the house from the previous owner, the Duke of Avonmouth and March.'

'The Duke of what?' exclaimed the celebrity, shaking his head to clear it.

'You heard,' said Stillway, raising his voice, as Doris came out attracted by all the shouting.

'Look,' said the celebrity, 'I think there must be some mistake. I know this house and no Duke has ever owned it, I assure you.'

Stillway went white.

'What are you telling me?' he said, a tremor in his voice. 'I paid a million and a half pounds for the hall and its contents and gave the owner Geoffrey March, the Duke, my cheque in exchange for the deeds. He drove off not two hours ago in fact, with his butler, in his old Fiat.'

The other man leaned on the bonnet of the blood-red Ferrari and smiled charmingly, mirth dimpling his cheeks. 'Any man who believes he can expect to get ten million pounds worth of priceless and irreplaceable antiques for a million and a half must either be the biggest fool in Christendom, or else fresh out of the looney bin,' he said, folding his arms.

'And you'd know the true value of this house's contents, would you?' asked James Stillway sarcastically.

The tanned celebrity laughed and nodded. 'I ought to, because I own it,' he said, dropping his bombshell. 'And I am sorry to say this but I think you've been conned by a very clever pair of jack-the-lads. Charles Frost, my ex-butler and Ronnie March my gardener. I'd given them both a week's notice for taking drugs in one of the estate cottages you see. The pair must be having a whale of a time on your million and a half quid, don't you think?'

'But I've got the deeds,' blustered Stillway, beside himself with fury. 'And, a solicitor called David something or other of the local firm Croxley's drew up the signed contract in the presence of my wife as a witness. Even if what you say is true I can still claim the building and its contents as mine because any court would agree that I bought in good faith.'

'That would be true normally,' said the celebrity, 'except for one thing.'

'What's that then?'

'You see, Charles's brother has a law degree and has until very recently worked at Croxley's training to be a notary and drawing up legal documents, with free access to the authentic water-marked official paper. And I am afraid old chap, that his name just happens to be David!'

Catching the Tide at the Flood

The wood was quiet and peaceful and normally untroubled by man, full of shadows and dark places even on the hottest of summer days; yet sunlight shone down brightly into the clearings and onto the meandering sandy paths and tracks that laced through it from innumerable directions, formed by deer and other creatures over many centuries. For this was an ancient woodland, devoid of conifers, and filled with broad-leafed hazel and ash trees, gnarled oaks and tall sycamores.

In the middle of the largest clearing stood the composer, humming a tune of his own devising and deep in thought with his head nodding as he walked along, oblivious alike to the day of the month as well as to the bird calls in the tops of the trees all about him.

He was a man of middle height, with silver hair which had been allowed to grow and thicken into a shapeless mane, he wore gold-framed spectacles above an aquiline nose and prim mouth, an Austrian by birth.

Feeling weary from being up all night writing on sheets of manuscript and also from the sapping heat of the sun, he flopped down at last on a rotting tree stump that crumbled slightly as he lowered his body down into a sitting position, by a little ribbon of stream.

Here he sat gazing into the trickling water and found the sound it made, and its coolness, refreshing. He would have stayed there forever but for what happened next which took him completely aback.

'You cannot stop but must go on as yet,' said a voice. A watery voice that seemed to come from the very stream below him.

'Remember time,' the voice went on. 'Remember all your times, and grieve, as time itself must grieve.'

The composer's shaggy eyebrows shot up and he couldn't help but imagine that his mind had snapped. He lowered his head into his open hands and sighed deeply as a small roe buck crashed through the ferns over to his right, and a cloud temporarily blocked out the sun.

'You will know why soon,' the voice said, when the sun came out brightly again with dazzling stars and auras, forcing the composer to shield his pale eyes with a cupped hand.

'What will I know?' he asked at last, bowing to the inevitability of co-operating with his obvious insanity.

But the water chuckling over the rocks and into overflowing pools yielded no further voice and all he heard was the insistent humming of the bees, and all he saw from then on until he left to go back to the house above the clipped lawns was the sunshine in an empty blue sky.

But the memory and the words of the voice continued to nag him all that evening, and he resolved to visit the clearing on the next hot dry summer day that came along, sensing that the voice would not speak in rain or the dullness that must follow on from searing heat.

It rained for two weeks solid without a break.

Yet the strange voice that seemed half in his head but outside of it too, continued to taunt him in all but his noisiest hours, and especially in the quietest time of the long night, when he tried to do his best work.

Then at last came a sunny day and he went to the ancient wood without delay. The time was an hour before midday and the sun was climbing up the east face of the sky, when he went to the crumbling tree stump and sat down, looking deep into the stream.

'Are you there?' he said out loud, feeling foolish and half afraid. 'Are you there today, at all? If so, please say so, for I am very interested in what you have to say, and we can help each other.'

The stream trickled its way over the mosses and the shelves of rock unhindered as he sat there and after some time had passed he felt forced to speak to the unknown voice again.

'Hello,' he said at length. 'My name is Anton Weiss. I am a composer who came to Great Britain just before the war, and have remained here ever since. I have a wife called Elise, who at 61, is thirteen years younger than I am and two children called Heidi and Franz - both thirty-five, they're twins. Would it be presumptuous of me to ask who you are? After all, I think that you owe me at least that, since I have told you everything, in a very general sense, about me.'

Another fifteen to twenty minutes passed but there was no answer, and by eight p.m. he had given up.

The next day, though there was a light drizzle which you sometimes get in the middle of August, for God is not merciless, he returned to the stump in his mac and sat under an umbrella. 'Is there anybody there?' he said, and immediately smiled inwardly at a distant memory of playing with a Ouija Board, in a friend's house without his parents' knowledge, when he was very young.

The stream, more swollen now, plunged and foamed and eddied, but did not speak, and he sighed and picked up a crooked stick and threw it in, letting the metal shaft of the umbrella rest against his right shoulder.

There seemed nothing else to do and he couldn't force an unseen voice to talk back to him for it was an entirely ridiculous situation in his view anyway, and about as unproductive and thankless as trying to train a cat to walk along a tightrope and sing. Disgusted, he got up and glared down at the stream.

'I shall not forget this rebuff,' he said with dignity, and made to go back to the house.

'You will be what you are,' said the voice suddenly. 'You will be who you say you are, but not who you think you are. The same as the birds and the water voles.'

The composer stood stock still and waited until the voice had finished. Then he spoke himself, appealing to its decency and higher motives as best he could.

'You have tormented me with your first round of speaking, and by not speaking since, until now. I have to point that out to you. Do you understand?'

'The sea, the wind, and all disasters that shall arise from the same source, all this shall be beyond the comprehension of many. Yet all books will be written, prayers said, and trembling hands will hold each other, when all that needs to be done is to accept and believe,' came from the stream.

'What must be believed?' asked Anton Weiss carefully, for he did not wish to offend the voice, or that it should go before he was ready, like last time.

A few seconds went and then the voice came again in the hushed and neutral tones it employed when addressing him a mere member of a useless and selfish race which could make rockets that shot to great heights in space, but couldn't supply a reason for this voice.

'Know this,' the voice said, breaking into his private thoughts. 'Long times can be short and brief days made briefer by knowledge of impending ends.'

'Yes? What does that mean, my dear friend?' he asked. But the conversation on a higher plane, if that is what it could be called, stopped there, and the voice had slipped away of its own volition once again.

This time he stayed by the stream, repeatedly asking it to respond to his entreaties but the only effect was the sound of the water running smoothly over its moss-covered rocks, and darkness falling rapidly as night approached. The white-haired composer was so long in the wood that his wife had to come and look for him, angry that her meal of halibut had burned.

The composer waited a week and then went back to the stream in the wood and sat down once again on the tree stump, slippery and damp from last night's heavy rain, though it had left off now - leaving only dripping leaves and muddy pathways underfoot.

'I will just sit here and not say a word,' vowed Anton Weiss to himself. 'Then maybe this voice will make itself heard again. And even if it speaks to me I shall not say anything in reply. I'll just keep quiet and listen, and see what happens.'

What happened was that the stream, fed and made stronger by the volume of the recent heavy rain and storms, boiled up and surged speedily down over its mossy bed, and a pale grey muddy hand emerged and grabbed the composer's trouser leg, trying to pull him down and in.

He got up quickly, digging in his heels and striking out with his closed umbrella at the relentless pull of the strange hand, the thick arm of which was covered in green and gold scales under the silt and the mud.

Although the umbrella was smashed in the process, so that it was useless for its intended purpose any more, the scaly arm and hand withdrew, and he scuttled away from the edge of the bank.

It had been a close shave and now he knew what manner of creature owned that voice. It was a stream monster of immense strength and size, and entirely carnivorous.

He would not go back to the ancient wood and the stump by the stream anymore. He would stay away and write the score of a brand new piece; a toccata and fugue for a thousand piece orchestra. And when he'd finished he would sell the house and move with his wife to another as far away as possible. It was the only thing to do, or he knew the god of the woodland stream would destroy his last remaining threads of sanity, or kill him.

* * * *

Eighteen months later, after he had moved to Ascot, and following the evening's performance of his new work aided by the Boston Philharmonic Orchestra, which he conducted himself, a beaming music critic came up to him and shook his hand.

'I'm from *The Times*, maestro,' he said, 'and I don't think I have ever heard a more inspired and evocative piece of music than that which I did tonight. Tell me, I'd be very interested to know. Where did you get your inspiration for 'The Water Vines'?'

'I can easily tell you that,' said Anton Weiss drily. 'It came to me when I happened to be having a pee in a wood and heard voices, and thought I'd been seen by two ladies. Thankfully, I had not. Please excuse me, but my wife is beckoning urgently to me, and wishes to go home. She is not a lover of music at all you know, and only comes to my concerts to humour me.'

'What did that man say to you Anton? He looks very confused, one might even say angry,' said Elise Weiss, buttoning up her sensible brown suede gloves.

'Oh him?' replied the composer. 'Just some fellow desperate to sell a house with a swimming pool. Of course, I said no, but he insisted that the pool could speak!'

Garden of Remembrance

In the cold November sunshine the French general stood in full uniform and with head bowed, before a grave in the war cemetery in northern France.

The well-kept grave had no name save 'an unknown soldier of the Great War', and the scruffy man trimming the hedge just across from the distinguished looking white-haired army officer, looked puzzled. Why should a full general pay his respects to an ordinary soldier whom now nobody could identify? 'Are you perhaps talking to your son, monsieur?' he called over, setting down the clippers.

The old man in the sky-blue uniform with rows of medal ribbons, and gleaming cavalry boots, looked up. 'No, not my son,' he said quietly. 'Just one of those I had the privilege to serve with at Verdun. There were so many young men like him who laid down their lives that France might remain free.'

The cemetery workman wiped his hands on his crumpled overall and came closer, planting his feet on the gravel in front of the general. 'Yes,' he said sneeringly. 'So many slaughtered like sheep, and for what? I served myself in a rifle company and saw many die, victims not so much of the Bosche, but of the donkeys behind them.'

'Donkeys? What donkeys?' said the general, looking at him.

The man in the overall shrugged and spat on the gravel at the general's feet. 'The incompetents at Headquarters I refer to,' he fumed. 'The doddering old fools who couldn't have organised a children's birthday party if they'd tried.'

'Where did you serve, my friend?' asked the general.

'At the Chemin des Dames and at Arras.'

'And your rank?'

'Only a private, like the dead man.'

The general nodded. 'A lot of families lost someone, that is the nature of war. But I don't think that you can say the commanders at H.Q. were all incompetents. Some may have been, but to say they all were is to display great ignorance without knowing the full facts.'

'Of course it was incompetence!' snapped the man in the overall challengingly. 'Those dead-beats with their straggling grey moustaches, and their upper-class idiot brains, skulking in comfort 30 miles behind the fighting and suffering in the trenches. You are an officer and must have seen it.'

'So you think that all of the generals were upper class snobs intent on getting the lower classes killed, with unworkable and ridiculous plans, just to promote their reputations?' said the general. 'No doubt there is more to your view than meets the eye. Are you perhaps political?'

'I am a communist, yes,' said the other man with fierce pride. 'I loathe and despise the rich parasites who get us into wars for their own ends. Such scum as that should be given a rifle and made to face the machine-guns like we did. There'd be no more wars then, I can promise you, monsieur.'

'I came originally from a poor family,' said the general, 'my father was a cobbler. I held high command during the war so you can hardly blame upper-class snobbery for everything.'

'You are different,' snapped the man, 'even though you are an officer. But let me tell you this, we humble ordinary soldiers were able to beat the idiots at H.Q. when things got bad. They didn't know what to do and you should have seen them panic.'

'What did you do then, to defeat your superiors?'

'What did we do? I will tell you. I was one of the main organisers of the mutiny when whole divisions laid down their guns and refused to fight. We demanded better treatment and food, more leave and more pay.'

'And did you get them?'

'Yes, but many men were court-martialled - 23,000 in all - and over 400 sentenced to death.'

'So what sort of a victory is that, even if you got your demands, if many of your comrades were executed, and branded as cowards?'

'A great victory over the hated ruling classes, monsieur, that was the main thing. In any conflict there are casualties. But the generals who were incompetents we didn't mind so much, it was the butchers. Ones like Huguenet, who took great pleasure in setting up firing squads to shoot the mutineers. He was present at every execution and read out the sentence. If I could ever kill him I would die happy. This Huguenet - he was the one whose failed attack gave me this mutilation on my neck.' He unbuttoned his shirt and showed the badly stitched-up bayonet wound.

The general paused and reached into his pocket, pulling out a wallet which he flipped open. 'I know it isn't much,' he said, 'but please take this for your pain. And don't imagine that all of your officers were brain-dead butchers.'

The cemetery gardener's eyes opened wide. 'No, you are different, monsieur,' he said, taking the thick wad of folded francs. 'You are a true gentleman of France. Why, there is enough here to buy a new car! Thank you, monsieur.'

The general walked away to the far end where the cemetery's ornamental gates stood open, and his car and chauffeur waited.

'Wait a minute, monsieur, what is your name?' called out the man in overalls urgently.

'My name is General Huguenet,' he said, getting into the limousine and slamming the door.

Russian Roulette

The Russian Marshal pored over the Soviet battle plan for the invasion of the United Kingdom and frowned. There were still not enough 'sleeping agents' yet in place to give aid to the regular forces in the event of air and ground attack, to tamper with communications, create the necessary chaos and internal disorder, and destroy civilian morale with sabotage and the spreading of false information.

There was a sharp knock on his office door and a uniformed aide entered and saluted smartly. The Marshal looked up, eyeing the paper in the man's hand. 'Yes, Colonel. What is it? You can see I am very busy at the moment. Whatever you have there to show me, I'm sure it can wait.'

'I don't think this can, sir,' said the intelligence Colonel. 'It has just come in from the President's office.'

'Very well, then. Place it in the tray on my desk and take yourself off. I must have peace and quiet for what I'm doing. Can you inform the heads of the Army, Navy and Air Force, that I wish to see them right away?'

'But sir,' blinked the Colonel. 'What about the dispatch from the Kremlin?'

'It can wait,' snapped the Marshal. 'Now vanish, Colonel. That's an order.'

Marshal Huntskaya addressed the assembled Chiefs of the military under his command gravely, outlining the deficiencies in the War Plan. 'Colonel-General Petrov, what is our current state of readiness, in terms of fully- equipped divisions, in the event of a threat against our country?'

'It is hard to say,' said the old man.

Huntskaya's face hardened.

'What do you mean?' he demanded.

'I mean, sir, that in the event of mobilisation we can call on maybe 5 million men who are still placed on the official reserve list. Whilst the present peace-time strength of our armies is in excess of 400 divisions, not counting airborne units, and support.'

'Tanks, General?'

'At the moment, approximately 15,000 of the new Mishka type introduced last year, and there are a number of older models such as the Bearcat and Shomilov T34s, but their numbers are negligible because they are being phased out. You may remember, sir, that we are still recovering from Afghanistan - and some of the tanks I have mentioned are at present on tours of duty in Bosnia, to protect the Serbs.'

'Artillery and Missile Carriers, General Petrov?'

'The same, about 15,000.'

'Thank you, General Petrov. Admiral Spannick, how many surface vessels with nuclear capability do the Royal Navy have?'

'The British? Far fewer than us. But their deep-water submarine fleet is formidable and can be considered significant.'

'Yet the British army scarcely has 200,000 men,' retorted the Marshal, to counter this oblique dent to Russian might. He looked at Air Marshal Fedor Mikoyan, the oldest man in the room, and a man he didn't like.

'What has our glorious Air Force to say?' he said suddenly, catching the 83 year old off guard.

'I can tell you very little, because I do not have the relevant papers with me,' replied the old man huffily, after a long pause.

'Don't you?' said Huntskaya. 'Then you're sacked!'

Later on, while he was cosied up with his latest mistress and feeding her black grapes and drips of vodka with his pudgy fingers, the red telephone buzzed stridently at his elbow and he snatched it up.

'Yes, this is Marshal Huntskaya. Who is that?

'Yes, Air Marshal Alexkov?

'When was this known?

'But this is catastrophic! Why wasn't I informed at once? How many? Never mind, Alexkov, send up everything we've got at once, do you hear? Fighters, Missiles, the new Flamedogs, the lot - and commit all, yes all, of our nuclear bombers in one huge simultaneous strike on New York, San Francisco, Los Angeles, Chicago and the Pentagon. Right! Don't just sit there, get it done, and report back when you have.'

He slammed the secret channel receiver down with a flushed face.

'What is it?' asked the girl.

'I have no time to talk,' said the Marshal, looking worried. 'I have to go to Moscow airport right away to be ready to control operations from the skies. The Americans have beaten us to the punch. Unbelievable, isn't it? My new replacement for the Air Force, a good man, Alexkov, and very alert. His staff using the new computer radar technology, have spotted nine fighters and a massive uniden-tified craft crossing Federation air space and heading for our capital! It's Armageddon come true!'

Boris Yeltsin, the Russian leader, stood on the tarmac in the pouring rain, alongside the Foreign Minister, with his coat collar pulled up and looking stern. 'Ah,' he said, looking round at the commotion of slamming jeep doors and running commandos, elbowing people out of the way with the butts of their weapons. 'Marshal? What are you doing here - and what an entrance!'

Huntskaya outlined what he knew, and asked for orders. 'What shall I do now, sir?' he asked the huge Yeltsin who stood looking at him impassively.

'Do, Marshal? Forgive me, but I thought I just heard you say that you had committed our great country to an irreversible thermonuclear war. What can one do in such circumstances?'

The Marshal paled. 'But, Mister Yeltsin,' he pleaded. 'You must give me some definite plan to work with. Nine Stealth fighters and the big bomber type we didn't know the U.S. possessed, will be flying over the outskirts of the city at any moment! The last report said they were flying at four times the speed of sound. You have to give me appropriate orders, or else take on the whole awesome responsibility yourself!'

'The responsibility, such as it is, is yours!' growled Yeltsin. 'I may as well tell you though, the nine planes and the larger one flying from America and speeding into our air space comprise the long-awaited state visit of President Clinton and his wife Hilary. You got us into this mess - so you get us out of it!'

The Homecoming

Colonel Clem Jefferson climbed down from the hay cart in a cloud of choking dust and thanked the driver.

Sweat was clinging to his threadbare shirt and his naked feet were caked with the accumulated grime of months of captivity.

It was high summer in Baxter County and the fiery sun was at its most dazzling at noonday.

'You in the war?' asked the carter, regarding him shrewdly and making no attempt yet to whip his horses on.

'Why yes, I fought in the last battle before the surrender at Appomattox, where we laid down our arms after five long years of fighting the Yankees.'

'I hate and despise Yankees,' said the man on the cart, leaning forward and spitting in the dust. 'You with the Army of Northern Virginia then - one of Lee's boys?'

'That's right, I volunteered right off. Why d'you ask anyway?'

'No reason, but you'll find things a bit changed around here. This your home town?'

'Yes, I have a farm just over yonder. A twelve acre spread, about three miles out of town.'

'A farm you say? Then I guess you'll be alright, 'cepting the Yankees will have run off all your stock and stolen everything that's edible. It was the big houses, owned by rich folks, that suffered most. Sherman's bandits took torches to them all, just out of badness. Even old Judge Binnion's place.'

Colonel Jefferson gaped at him and shook his head. 'Old Judge Binnion? But why? I never met a fairer or a gentler man in the whole of my life. And, what's more, a man who refused to take sides, either North or South; he was so determined to remain neutral and not get dragged into things. That's truly terrible, and I can hardly believe it.'

'Hung the old man as well,' said the carter.

'No!'

'Yep. Strung him up on a tree by the gates of his own house. Said he was a southern spy. Hung him in front of his children and two little babies, God strike them down, and do the same.'

'As I say, that's terrible. I hope one day that the guilty men are found and punished.'

The carter sneered and spat on the ground again. 'What rank were you in the Confederate Army, anyway?'

'A full Colonel.'

'What age are you?'

'Twenty-nine.'

'That's a might young. You must have been a very brave man to have been promoted a full Colonel, at your age.'

'I don't know about that. Mind you, my hair wasn't grey when I signed up, but it sure is now!'

'What will you do now? You got young 'uns?'

'Yes I have. Though they'd be grown some now. When I left Ben was nine, well he'll be going on fourteen now. And Sarah was six, while little Samuel was no higher than your boot, and just a babe in arms'

'I've got to go now, Colonel. See you, and good luck.'

The paroled Southern Colonel watched the cart creak crookedly down the main street, kicking up dust with its slanted wheels, and went on to what used to be the Bank, though it was hard to tell now - the building was almost a derelict ruin.

A small round man came out from the back and peered shortsightedly at him through the security bars. 'Yes, can I help you? Do you have an account here? If so, you are wasting your time, the whole damned country is broke and overdrawn, and there's not a dollar in the place.'

'I see,' said Colonel Jefferson. 'I did used to have an account, but I haven't come about that. I don't suppose you know my wife, do you? Her name is Ellen Jefferson.'

'I'm a stranger,' said the man. 'Sent from Richmond to try and sort things out. Not making much progress though; the conquerors burned all the records, and blew up the safe.'

'Thank you, I'll try elsewhere.'

He went back out to the sun-drenched main street again.

Outside, he continued walking along to the end of town. Then he saw the Reverend Polk, and gave a cry of joy.

'Reverend. You remember me, don't you? Clem Jefferson, the husband of Ellen Jefferson. You baptised both our eldest children, Ben and Sarah, just before the war.'

The Baptist Minister's eyes clouded over and he gazed off into the distance. 'So many years of war. There have been so many deaths and so much hardship. I'm sorry, what you say means nothing to me. It's hard for me to remember five minutes ago, let alone something that happened so many years before. The war has revealed the militant side of God, my friend, and it is only by His divine providence that you and I are able to stand here in peace, and untroubled by bloody misfortune.' He put his hand to his eyes and pinched them, then let his arm drop again, and gave a wan smile. 'You must forgive me, I have to go and visit the widow of John Foster - he's just died of wounds he received at Gettysburg.'

'Say, Reverend, I was present at Gettysburg too.'

'That may be son, that may be. But the main thing is you're here right now, and still able-bodied and strong, unlike so many who have suffered - women and children, and old men. Strong men like you will be needed more than ever now to reconstruct a new South on the ashes of the old. Men have sinned, and have paid the price, which was heavy. God has rested from His labour of destruction at last, and fields may yet bloom again with the bounty of the harvest. Else, famine will make a visitation, and strike down hard, as it did on the Egyptians in the time of Pharoah.'

The scenes that met his eyes now as he travelled further were terrible to contemplate, and he began to fear for his family, for the first time.

Stranded negro servants in tatters of clothes, and some entirely naked, roamed like wild animals, eating garbage, or weeping abjectly by the side of the trail.

An elderly gentlewoman who had lost her mind waylaid him staring from out of her straggly unkempt loose hanging hair, and pointed an accusing finger, calling out in a shrill voice: 'Have you seen my jewellery? You came to my house when I was in bed and broke open my lovely bookcase. Then you stabbed my husband, and clubbed him to the ground. He's still lying on the floor where you left him - dead and unburied. Even though the flames consumed the room itself, yet he lives on.'

Her face took on a crafty look as she moved closer and grabbed his shirt, clawing his chest with her long filthy nails. 'Took his gold Hunter, that his Daddy had given him, didn't you? Think I don't know? Have you seen my pretty jewellery, sir? Have you seen my jewellery, I had it not five minutes ago.'

He gently prised her stained and dirty fingers from his shirt, and a tall negro stepped forward. 'I'll look after Missus Greenslade now, sah. Yankee renegades done give her a bad time. Raped her daughter and all, and the old lady herself. Terrible thing, sah. A terrible thing...'

Now, urgency lent wings to fear and he literally ran the last half mile, and then relaxed when he saw the weather-boarded farmhouse. It was untouched and crops grew in the fields, and the old plough horse neighed with recognition.

Flinging aside his ragged shirt he walked proudly and bare-chested up the driveway between the well-constructed paddocks of hickory wood, resting his hand on the reassuring solidness of the seasoned timber. Then the front door of the two-storey house with the veranda stood before him for the taking.

Yet now, after almost four and a half years absence, a painful shyness became all-powerful, and he tiptoed away, like a thief, deciding to come back before nightfall, when he estimated he'd be more ready to face the better memories of the past.

When the sun went down and dusk cloaked the town and the fields he returned up the drive, steadier but still as bashful and unsure of himself as a youth meeting a girl for the first time.

Instead of knocking, and making himself known, or throwing open the front door, he sidled across to look in one of the downstairs windows to see if he could see his wife, or the three children that were strangers to his love.

His eyes gradually became used to the dark interior through the cool glass pane and he spoke in a low voice, out loud. 'If I might look on her sweet face again and know that she is happy.'

A fire burned brightly in the hearth of the room he looked into, flickering its reflection from the mahogany furniture. Then the burnished cups and silver on the sideboard did their own talking. They were not his, or hers either, and entirely unfamiliar. With a feeling of sick panic he hurried around the back of the house and stared through the window there.

Yes, there was a young boy and girl, older now, but still recognisable as his eldest son and beloved daughter. But, where was Ellen, and the baby, though the baby would be a little boy now, of about five and a half.

His daughter Sarah was laughing and showing off a silver bracelet and tears pricked his eyes. He had never been able to give her things like that. How had her mother managed to do it, and why was his house one of the few untouched? He thought of the scenes of desolation he'd seen in the town and on the way there, contrasted all, and felt a great sadness. His farm was much as it had been when he'd left with high hopes of winning glory, being shot at for a dollar a day, and it wasn't right. There were no marks of suffering here.

A voice he knew sounded and Ellen came in. She was talking to someone, and then the middle-aged man in the blue uniform of a Union major followed, holding Samuel in his arms.

'My God,' he breathed. His wife no more and a stranger - an enemy stranger come to that - taking the love of small children that was not his by natural right.

Mixed emotions formed in conflict in his tortured mind. Great sacrifices of bravery and heroism, he had seen, days of hunger and having to do without, fond memories of Ellen, and now this...

Not trusting his self-possession, he walked softly away just as darkness was falling. Swiftly, and without even stopping to calm his seething mind, he acted. Took out the gun he had in the waistband of his grey uniform trousers with the pale yellow stripe down the seams and put it in his mouth, and pulled the trigger.

Inside the house, yet far away enough not to hear the fateful shot, Ellen Jefferson took her son from the man and reminded her daughter Sarah to put the new silver bracelet away back into the drawer before it got lost. 'It's valuable darling. Worth over forty dollars, and Uncle Jake didn't give it to you just so you could misplace it carelessly. Oh, Jake?'

'Yes, my dear?'

'It's the strangest thing, but I had a letter from Clem last week, the first for many months. It had become all crumpled and torn during its journey but the writing, and the message it contained, was clear.'

'What did the letter say, Ellen?'

'It was a note to say that Clem was coming home and that he'd be back sometime today, but he hasn't come.'

The man stroked his bushy side-whiskers and smiled. 'From what you have told me about Clem, his arrival won't be delayed very long. He loves you Ellen, and a love as strong as that cannot help but lend flight to a man's heels. Clem will find a way here real soon, never fear.'

She frowned deeply.

'Clem has been through so much, you know, and the letter was sent from the prison camp at Fort Monroe. Life cannot be easy there, not for the officers, nor the men.'

'You forget that I too, was, for a short time at least, and in the early years of the war, a prisoner of the South. Locked up in a guarded tobacco warehouse in Richmond. Until I was swopped during the exchange, before President Lincoln stopped all that.'

He paced up and down in front of her for a moment and then leant his elbow on the mantelpiece above the fire, staring out the window.

'I always thought it strange, and the supreme irony, that here we are, brother and favourite sister, and yet you married a Southern Colonel with his own regiment fighting in Georgia, while I served on the other side, as an aide to the Northern Commander-in-Chief, General Ulysses S. Grant. The other irony of course, was that I never met him.'

Showdown

The police had chased the bank robbers to the two-storey house in the suburbs, the two robbers had smashed down the front door, and then called out from an upstairs window that they intended keeping the family inside hostages.

An armed response unit was called in and police cars sealed off all the roads. Later on a skilled negotiator arrived from the Home Office, together with some soldiers from the S.A.S., sporting heavy machine guns and stun grenades.

'Who is the senior officer here?' asked the negotiator.

'I am,' said a uniformed Superintendent, ducking under some striped plastic tape, and stepping forward.

'Well, what's the score so far?'

'Two white males robbed a bank in town and then holed up in the house. Both of them are known to be armed with sawn-off shotguns and revolvers.' He eyed the S.A.S. men standing in groups talking and grinned. 'Shall we rush the place and go in hard?'

'Don't do anything of the kind,' said the negotiator. 'How much did they get?'

'About fifty thousand, plus the contents of some security boxes in the vaults.'

'And who are they holding in the house?'

'We don't know sir, but the neighbours say two sisters and a little boy live there, middle-aged ladies, I believe sir.'

'How old's the boy? Do you know?'

'Yes sir. I'm told he is about four.'

The negotiator nodded. 'Could be tricky. Any demands yet?'

'No, as quiet as the grave. The men just shouted down to us that they were holding the people who live in the house and keeping them hostage.'

'Have they threatened to shoot them?'

'No sir, not yet. You don't think it'll come to that, do you?'

The negotiator shrugged. 'You never know with this type of men when they are desperate,' he said.

'We've managed to rig up a telephone line to the villains,' said the Superintendent. 'Do you want to speak to them now?'

'Yes, ring through. It's important that we set up contact as soon as possible so as to get a rapport going. The text book theory is that it is somehow harder to kill a person when you've spoken to them than when they are just an anonymous stranger, so to speak.'

The Superintendent nodded. 'Very well sir. Right, here's the handset. One of them is on the other end. You can speak now, sir.'

'Hello, am I speaking to the men who are holding people hostage in number three Abander Close?'

'That's right, mate. We've got two women and a little boy. We won't hurt them if you lot do as I say. First of all, I want the street cleared of filth cars, and some food and cigarettes brought by somebody neutral, like a woman neighbour.'

'Anything else?'

'Yeah. A helicopter to land on the lawn in two hours, and a pilot who won't play tricks, and who has a healthy respect for his life - you got me? We've got plenty of guns you know; we are fully tooled-up, and we've lots of spare ammo.'

'I know that,' said the negotiator calmly. 'Can you promise that no-one will be harmed?'

'Not if you do what we say.'

'It'll take a few hours more than you've allowed us to get a helicopter,' said the negotiator. 'The food and cigarettes are another matter, and I'll arrange it now. But, listen, the women and the little boy, they are not to be harmed, do you understand. I am very firm on that.'

'I'm ringing off now,' snarled the voice. 'Get our chopper here in two hours or the first person will be shot. I'm not joking mate. You are playing God with people's lives if you even think of playing me false.'

The food asked for was taken in by a young policewoman in jeans and a red sweater. When she returned, the Superintendent asked her if she had seen any of the men inside.

'No, sir,' she said. 'The man inside the house shouted instructions at me through the letter box and told me to leave the tray and get away, which I did.'

'Was that all he said?'

She looked uncomfortable, and coloured slightly, before answering. 'No sir. He also asked me what size bra I had on.'

'Well done, lass,' said the Superintendent looking grim. 'Sergeant Baynes!' he called to the leader of the armed response team. 'Can you get your men to take a bead on those upstairs windows before it gets dark. They'll put the lights on and maybe cast their shadows on the curtains. There's only two, and we might be able to down them and rush the house suddenly.'

'Don't be a fool,' said the Home Office negotiator. 'The lives of the hostages are in our hands man, and the world's press are watching.'

'Well, they might have got free sandwiches and pop,' said the Superintendent, 'but that's all they'll get, if I'm in charge. No way are they getting their other demand for a helicopter.'

'I am in charge, as a matter of fact,' said the negotiator.

The Superintendent looked shame-faced.

'I was talking about the police operations, sir,' he said.

Two hours later the telephone rang and the negotiator snatched it up.

'Where's this bleeding helicopter?' asked a voice.

'It's coming,' he said. 'There's a lot of air traffic about at the moment from Heathrow'.

'You wouldn't be fooling me, would you?' said the voice.

'No, I wouldn't try anything like that, because I fear for those two ladies and the boy. Can't you at least let the boy go, he is innocent after all, and it isn't the act of a big man to hold a gun on a defenceless child of four.'

'Watch it. You are treading out of bounds,' said the bank robber. 'I tell you what I'll do, I'll let one of the women out, but that's all, to show my good faith. But, I am hanging on to the other one and the boy, they are my only chance of getting out of this.'

'All right,' said the negotiator, slowly. 'Send her now, and I'll tell the armed police to stand back.'

The front door opened and a woman in a green and white frock and headscarf emerged, crying and looking frightened. A policeman rushed over and pulled her to safety. She was brought to the mobile police H.Q.

'You all right, madam?' asked the Superintendent. 'They didn't harm you, did they?'

The woman shook her head.

'How's the little boy?' he asked gently.

But the woman broke down and sobbed into her hands, so that he couldn't make out what she said. He beckoned to two paramedics.

'She's in shock,' he said. 'Take her off to hospital. We can get her statement later.'

The ambulance roared off with its siren wailing, carrying the middle-aged woman to hospital. The telephone rang again. The man on the other end sounded impatient and angry.

'What about my helicopter?' he demanded. 'You said it would be here an hour ago. I've released one hostage, so how about you doing something your end?'

'Nothing doing,' said the Superintendent, into the handset. 'You horrible men give yourselves up, do you hear?'

'Get lost, copper!' said the man, and the line went dead again.

'Superintendent,' said the negotiator. 'I'll take over. You will end up getting the remaining hostages and most of your men killed, that way.'

Powerful arc lights were drenching the close in brightness, and they picked up a figure in khaki combat fatigues and a motorcycle crash helmet as he leaned down from the windowsill of the besieged semi, and dropped something. The police marksmen tensed, but the negotiator waved his hand warningly.

'I'll see what he's sent us,' he said, and ran over and picked the object up from the grass.

'It's a child's teddy,' he said slowly, as he brought it back to the police van. 'What do you think it means?'

'It means that we should have gone in a lot earlier,' said the Superintendent. 'All these psychological tactics are rubbish. Good old rough stuff is the only thing these villains understand, believe me. I have sorted out many a fight in the street, meeting violence, with violence, I can tell you.'

'Yes, but this is not an ordinary affray,' said the negotiator, 'and those men have guns and hostages. I know they will use the guns if provoked, and they know they can lose nothing by killing three or four policemen, before they themselves are killed.'

'They'd better not,' said the Superintendent darkly.

The negotiator rang through to the house again. The phone was immediately picked up.

'Are you there?' asked the negotiator.

'Don't be bloody stupid, of course I am,' answered the man on the other end. 'You've got this place completely surrounded.'

'Look, I can't get a helicopter,' he said. 'I have tried, but I can't. We are dealing with inter-service rivalries and red tape, you see. Neither the R.A.F. or the civil airlines will give me one. So you'll have to modify your demands somewhat. What about if I give you a police car instead and a guarantee of safe passage?'

'Too slow,' said the man laughing unpleasantly. 'But I tell you what, if you get us a brand-new Porsche or Jaguar XJ6 from some showroom then you have a deal.'

'I'll check with my superiors,' said the Home Office man, 'and ring back.'

Half an hour later he rang again. It was quite dark now and the lights made the suburban cul-de-sac look unreal, as if it was a film set during the shooting of an action movie. The phone was picked up.

'What's occurring?' said a voice.

'My superiors say, if you let one more hostage go, they will do as you wish, but you are to leave the little boy when you drive off.'

'How do I know I can trust you?'

'You don't, but I don't know if I can trust you either.'

'Okay, the woman will be released as soon as we see the car arriving,' said the man. 'But no tricks Mister, or the little boy will be in the morgue, along with us.'

'All right, the car will arrive in exactly two minutes. It is a 'Q' registration Porsche in metallic blue, with a smoked windscreen.'

'Right-oh.'

The line went dead again.

All the police and the S.A.S. men watched as a young driver parked the car on the lawn outside the house and got out holding up the ignition keys, before putting them into the ignition again, to show the watching villains the car was ready to go. Then the driver sprinted away.

'There's only half a gallon in it,' whispered the Superintendent. 'They'll get about five miles down the road, top whack.'

The house door opened, and true to the villain's word, another lady came out with her hands shielding her eyes. Two policemen went to her as she slithered about erratically in her carpet slippers, dazzled by the lights. The Superintendent asked them to let the neighbours look after the woman and get her out of the firing line.

'Right men,' he said quietly. 'Aim for their legs, and mind the little boy. They won't be long now. They can't get away.'

'What are they playing at?' he asked impatiently, half an hour later.

Some time after that the S.A.S. stormed the house with stun grenades and broke in with guns blazing. It was quite spectacular to watch these professionals with black overalls and knitted balaclavas go to work, the police outside and the civilians hemmed in behind the tape, let out huge cheers.

Inside it was a different story. The place was empty. No sign of the two men anywhere, or the boy. All that was left was a scribbled note on the tray asking if the villains could have cucumber sandwiches next time, instead of paste.

The Superintendent stalked around like an angry gander, shoving people out of the way and looking murderous. 'Those two women!' he roared loudly. 'Where are they!'

The Ringer

Lord Bentley watched critically as his brand new three year old bay colt was led into the yard by the trainer for his inspection.

'Here we are, my lord,' said Frank Butters proudly. 'Vaseline the Second, your champion contender for this year's Derby. Looks well, doesn't he?'

Lord Bentley pursed his lips primly and walked all around the colt frowning. He stooped down to examine a leg, and then stood up to his full height again, his eyes narrowing suspiciously.

'Is there something wrong, my lord?' asked Frank Butters.

'Yes,' said Lord Bentley acidly. 'This horse is not mine.'

The trainer blinked. 'Not yours, your lordship? This is Vaseline the Second, by Conan the Destroyer, out of Gadfly. I bought him for you at the Tattersalls Spring Sale in Newmarket. Surely, you have not forgotten?'

He turned to the lad patiently holding the colt's head. 'Lead him round again, Kelly. And this time don't rush, so his lordship can take his time.'

'Butters,' said Lord Bently coldly. 'This colt is not Vaseline, but some other horse entirely. My colt has three white legs, while this bay has none. I think you had better explain yourself...'

'Kelly,' said the trainer angrily. 'If you are playing one of your childish practical jokes you have picked the wrong time! What can you be thinking of, bringing out the wrong colt? Lord Bentley is this stable's greatest benefactor, by far, and he already has nine other mounts here. Your misplaced sense of humour will result in the sack if you don't pull yourself together man. Now, go and fetch Vaseline the Second at once. His lordship's time is valuable, and he hasn't driven all the way up here from his estate in Sussex, just to be mucked about by the likes of you. Go and get the right horse immediately!'

'Well, it was you who saddled him up and put the tack on,' said the stable lad resentfully. But a sharp look from the trainer had him leading the offending bay away.

Meanwhile, Frank Butters turned to Lord Bentley and made polite conversation to smooth down the ruffled feathers of the aristocrat whose vile temper and impatience with fools were legendary.

The trainer knew you didn't trifle with Lord Bentley, the humourless head of a vast banking empire, and Chief Steward of the Jockey Club. 'I am sorry about that, Sir,' he said, switching on a disarming smile. 'You just can't get the staff nowadays, that you could before the war.'

'Just get it right, Butters,' glowered the aristocrat, flicking a gob of manure and straw from an immaculate toe cap, with the pointed ferrule of his silver-chased walking cane.

'Ah, here is my man Kelly,' said the trainer brightening. 'But Kelly, where is his lordship's horse? Why have you come back empty-handed?'

Kelly shrugged, very red faced. 'Guv'nor, I think that you had better come and look for yourself. I can't find the blessed animal anywhere!'

Frank Butters quickly drew Kelly round, aware of Lord Bentley's fierce eyes on them both. 'Please be good enough to wait a moment my lord, and I will fetch him myself personally.'

Out of sight around the corner, the trainer grabbed the lad's jerkin sleeve roughly. 'Look here, Kelly,' he growled. 'What are you playing at? That's Lord Bentley there in the yard, and we can't afford to have him put out. Why are you doing this? Are you trying to make a fool out of me, because if you are, then by God you'll be sorry. And you can forget all about moving into Mulberry Cottage with your wife and six kids after this, I promise you.'

'Guv'nor, the horse isn't there. Not in the paddocks, the boxes, or anywhere, honest to God. He has simply disappeared into thin air. Perhaps he's been stolen.'

'Don't be ridiculous, Kelly. All the horses were there when I turned them out into the main paddock when the first string came back, and the second lot haven't started out yet. Come with me and we'll both look for him. He has to be somewhere.'

After an exhaustive search of the entire stable yard and grounds the trainer and the lad leaned despondently over a five-barred gate, looking at the twenty-odd thoroughbreds milling about in the paddock in front of them. 'You were right Kelly, the colt isn't here,' said the trainer. 'But we have to find him double-quick. We can't keep a man like Lord Bentley hanging about any longer. The trouble is, that while one or two of these colts here have one white leg, and some even have two, I can't see one anywhere with three!'

'That's what I told you, Guv'nor,' said Kelly. 'We'll just have to go to the owner and own up that we've lost him. There's no other way out.'

Frank Butters looked at him aghast. 'We can't do that. He'd have a purple fit. No, I've thought of an idea. Look, there's a bucket of whitewash and a brush by the wall of the haybarn. Go and get them for me, will you?'

The stable lad regarded him oddly. 'What are you going to do then, Guv'nor?'

'I am going to turn a bay colt with two white legs into one with three,' he said, smiling thinly.

'You can't do that, Guv'nor!'

'Oh, yes I can, Kelly, and I'm going to. That whitewash is a new kind that dries in seconds. I remember reading about it on the tin. But be quick before Lord Bentley takes it into his head to walk around the corner and catches us in the act. You go and get the whitewash and I will try to catch one of those younger colts with two white legs.'

With fingers crossed, they led the doctored colt back to where Lord Bentley waited, visibly furious, in front of the trainer's weathered limestone cottage.

'Here we are, my Lord,' said Butters cheerfully, wheeling the colt round by the bridle, with Kelly's help. 'Vaseline the Second at last.'

'That isn't my horse either!' snapped Lord Bentley icily. 'My horse has a white blaze shaped like a star on its forehead. This one does not.'

Frank Butters made a great show of examining the horse's head before again berating Kelly. 'I told you to fetch Vaseline the Second, didn't I?'

'Yes, you did, Guv'nor. I'm very sorry.'

'Sorry isn't good enough. You can see how angry his lordship is getting. Come with me and I will sort this out myself, because I cannot trust you to do the simplest thing.'

He thrust the reins into Kelly's hands and pushed him before him, along with the horse. 'I will be but a short while, my lord,' he added, bowing stiffly from the neck to the sour-faced owner, who took out a gold hunter and studied it pointedly.

Again the whitewash was hastily applied, and the trainer blew on his handiwork before throwing the wet brush back into its dented bucket. 'Not bad, even if I say so myself,' he declared, gesturing at the perfect star he had managed to create on the animal's head. But Lord Bentley disagreed.

'Do you take me for an idiot?' he demanded, waving his stick at them.

'What do you mean, sir?' asked the trainer in dismay. 'This must be your colt. Has he not three white legs, and a star-shaped blaze, just as you described?'

'Yes, he has,' said Lord Bentley grimly. 'But where is the crescent-shaped scar on his right ear described in the ownership papers?'

'Ah, yes of course,' replied the trainer, slapping his forehead theatrically. 'It's my fault and I do apologise, Lord Bentley. You see, the mix-up occurred because for some reason this season, we seem to have a lot of three year old colts with three white legs and star-shaped blazes in the yard, when you wouldn't normally see one in a blue moon. I can lay my hands on Vaseline the Second instantly, your lordship, because only one of the colts has a scarred ear. I saw him just now, as a matter of fact, when we were fetching this fellow out. I am truly sorry you have been so inconvenienced.'

Leaving the fuming aristocrat banging the end of his stick on the cobbles they went round the corner to the back, and the trainer stopped by a muddy puddle left over from the previous night's heavy rainstorm.

As Kelly watched, mystified, Butters bent his tweed-jacketed back and scooped up a handful of mud and stood up again, applying it to the colt's ear, frowning in concentration, and grunting with effort.

He finished and stepped back nodding his approval, throwing the surplus mud down and wiping his soiled hands clean on a handkerchief.

'What were you doing just now, Guv'nor?' asked Kelly, darting worried glances at the end corner of the building.

'Look for yourself, lad. Isn't that the finest crescent-shaped scar you have ever seen on the ear of a thoroughbred three year old?'

Kelly looked at the rapidly-drying mud and had to agree. 'You'd never guess unless you had been told,' he said admiringly. 'You never told me you were artistic kind Guv'nor. What you've done there is a very fine work of art, to be sure, and if you ever felt like giving up the training game there'd be a place for you at the Royal Academy, you can depend on that.'

Butters shot him a look but could detect no mickey taking. 'Right then,' he said briskly. 'Let's get this damned colt back without delay. He's caused us more than enough trouble as it is already, what with this surprise visit from the owner.'

Turning the corner into the yard again they were confronted by Tompkins-Gazeley, the work rider who rode all of the stable stars. He was sitting astride a bay colt with three white legs and a star-shaped blaze that could only be the real Vaseline the Second.

Yanking on the reins and skidding to a halt just in time, the trainer motioned with his hand for Kelly to take the colt with them, back, while he talked to the work rider. 'Have you seen Lord Bentley?' he asked.

The rider nodded. 'Yes, Guv'nor. He's just this moment driven off through the gates. I've just come back from buying fags in the village on Vaseline. Lord Bentley left you a message by the way. He said it was very important.'

'Message?' said the trainer. 'What message? Was his lordship pleased with how the colt looked when he saw him?'

'Not exactly, Guv'nor,' said the work rider lighting up a Woodbine with his free hand, and throwing the spent match down carelessly. 'Lord Bentley said to tell you that a horsebox and trailer would come and take his horses out of the yard sometime today and that you'd definitely be hearing from his solicitors in the very near future!'

Death of a Lady

It wasn't very easy cutting the body up with just a rusty hacksaw and a knife. James Crandle surveyed the results of his handiwork and shook his head.

There had been a lot more blood than he'd imagined when contemplating the act, and it had seeped through the inadequate layers of newspaper he had laid down on the front room carpet and had left a stain.

He would just have to spend further time, after packing the severed pieces of flesh and bone into the black plastic rubbish bag, scrubbing at the mark with washing up liquid.

His wife and daughter were asleep upstairs and they mustn't see it, or they'd begin asking questions.

Two hours later, just as the clock on the village church was striking three, James Crandle lugged the refuse bag out to his car, and placed it into the boot.

Then, casting a glance back at the darkened windows of the semi-detached house he fetched the rubber torch and a spade, from the garden shed, and slung them in the back, getting in.

The car was sluggish and took time to start, but a quarter of an hour later, he was driving up the deserted lane to the strip of isolated woodland where he planned to bury the remains.

As the bright headlights picked out the familiar boundary hedge and five-barred wooden gate he chuckled to himself.

Nobody was likely to discover the body for many years. The field belonged to a farmer who despised property developers, and though the man had had many attractive offers, he had stubbornly refused to sell. The farmer was unlikely to want to dig holes in his own field, he grew wheat, and his plough only disturbed the first four inches, or so, of topsoil, when it came to planting seed.

No, his secret was about as secure as any could be. And the best thing was, that Barbara his wife, and Tracey, his fourteen year old daughter, would never know what happened. That thought gave him intense satisfaction. And nobody would miss Milly anyway, or be likely to ask awkward questions.

To tell the truth, he had never liked Milly because she was so fat, though the rest of his family had found her company stimulating when she had arrived to stay from Scotland. His father, in particular, had viewed her as the apple of his eye.

Besides, he had told Barbara and Tracey that Milly had gone off on one of her regular jaunts, and they had believed him.

They were not to know that Milly had contracted cancer of the stomach, and that he had killed her by suffocating her the afternoon before, when they had both been out shopping.

He had hidden Milly's lifeless body in the loft, and had bided his time to dispose of her.

Now he had, and the feeling of release was wonderful.

Another thing too, before he had done Milly in, he hadn't known whether he could go through with something like that.

People in stories he had read about murderers always had horrible dreams, that in the end betrayed their secret crimes, but ever since he had smothered Milly on Saturday afternoon he had slept like an innocent baby. And he felt he could do it all again, if he had to ...

Nearing the house on the way back, he saw the man step out into the road, and put his arm up. He braked sharply and stared with sick fascination at the policeman in the bright glare of the car's lights.

'Just a routine check, sir, you are out very late. May I ask where you have just come from?'

James Crandle switched on a smile and hoped he didn't appear ill at ease, or nervous. This was all he needed, with blood and soil still on his hands, and the dirty spade and the used plastic bag flung carelessly into the boot.

'I have been to a party officer,' he lied. 'To tell you the truth I am glad to be going home. It was a very dull party full of snobs, and silly, unattached middle-aged women.'

He had meant that last bit as a sort of lighthearted joke between men, but the policeman continued to regard him sternly.

'Have you been drinking?' he asked knowingly. 'If you have just come from a party, then you must have had a couple. In fact now that I've leaned closer I can detect the smell of alcohol on your breath. I must ask you to take a breathalyser test.'

James Crandle swore under his breath.

He had had a drink. He had been forced to, because cutting up the body had been such an ordeal. The trouble was he had polished off at least five scotches ...

'I did have a small drink officer,' he said. 'But only one. I am an architect as a matter of fact, and as such, a responsible citizen. I know all about the risks in being over the limit at the wheel. Surely you can accept my word on this occasion.

'No sir,' said the constable firmly. 'I don't have a breathalyser kit on me, as I am not a traffic policeman, but I must ask you to come back to the station and we'll do the test there. Follow behind my patrol car, and I'll show you the way.'

James Crandle sat in the interview room looking pale. He had just been told that he was three times over the legal limit. In addition, the police had searched his car very thoroughly and found the spade and bloody plastic refuse sack; the red stains on his hands and shirt cuff had been obvious from the start in the brightly-lit reception.

Now he was not facing an ordinary constable, but a high-ranking pair of detectives who had been called from their beds and weren't best pleased. An attractive young policewoman in a tight-fitting uniform brought in three teas in polystyrene cups. One of these was pushed grudgingly across to the luckless prisoner.

'Cigarette?' asked one of the men questioning him.

James Crandle took the cigarette with shaking fingers, and allowed the detective to give him a light from a flaming petrol lighter.

'Well now,' said the detective grimly. 'About this spade with traces of fresh soil on, and the plastic bag. What can you tell us about those?'

It was no use lying, he could see that, and he was deep enough in trouble as it was.

'Look,' he said, fiddling with the cigarette in front of him. 'Can we do a deal, here?'

The detectives regarded him with narrowed eyes.

'What sort of deal?' the one who'd given him the cigarette asked.

'Well, you see, I have been doing some thinking. And if I tell you about what you've just asked, and show you where I have disposed of the body, will you consider dropping the drink-driving charge?'

They stared at him disbelievingly.

'Are you telling us that you admit burying a body with the spade we found, and that the body you refer to was carried to the scene of burial, in the black plastic sack, in the boot of your car?'

'Exactly. Well, do we have a deal or not? If you won't play ball, then I shall just have to fall back on my right of silence, and say nothing. That will cost you a lot of man-hours and money. A detailed search of a whole neighbourhood can't be that cheap, and besides I have buried the body in a very safe place, one you may never find.'

They looked at each other and then back at him. 'All right. It's a deal. Tell us about the body now.'

James Crandle smiled bleakly.

'Wait a moment. I'd have to see you tear up the constable's signed statement first, and insist that the breathalyser print out was destroyed.'

'You are clever,' said the detective with the cigarettes lighting up one for himself and laying the open packet down on the table in reach of the prisoner.

'Inspector Grey, see that all that is done, as Mister Crandle wants it, will you? And tell Constable 499 Lee, that tonight's nicking of the motorist never happened.'

'Milly was getting ill,' he dictated, as the more junior detective wrote it down. 'So partly because I felt sorry for her, and partly because I disliked the way she got around my wife, I did her in by holding a pillow over her head, while she was asleep, and sitting on it. She didn't struggle much, and the whole thing took no longer than the time it takes to boil an egg.'

'One moment sir. So you admit that you felt animosity towards this Milly?'

James Crandle nodded eagerly.

'Oh yes, I hated her all right, and she knew it.'

'Had you had an argument recently? A sudden falling out that prompted you to this extreme reaction?'

James Crandle laughed deeply.

'An argument? No I wouldn't exactly call it that. If we did, the talking was all one-sided. Milly couldn't talk back you see.'

'You mean she had some sort of speech impediment?' said the detective asking all the questions, in a shocked voice.

'No of course not, Superintendent, Milly was a Siamese Cat!'

Journey Without An End

The young squire sat in the conservatory, surrounded by green plants and orchids, going over the estate accounts with Daniel Macneice, his bailiff.

The squire sat forward making a church of his pale slim fingers, and nodded at the open ledgers in front of him. 'Well, how do we stand, Macneice?' he asked. 'Can I buy that new hunter or not?'

The bailiff met his eye from beneath his broad-brimmed felt hat. 'We stand fair over all sir. But some of the tenants are a bit behind with their rents. Though this, in turn, is balanced again by the sales of timber following the great gales in the spring.'

The master nodded, satisfied.

'There is something I wanted to ask you, Macneice.'

'Sir?'

'Do I pay you enough, do you think, for all you do?'

The bailiff flushed.

'I have no complaints, sir.'

The younger man nodded thoughtfully and got up from the table, going over to fondle the trailing vine hanging down from the trunk of a banana palm, and gazed up at the whitewashed high-vaulted ceiling.

'Do you know,' he said quietly. 'It has taken me the three years since my father died to fully realise that he is dead. Before that, even last month, I imagined I could hear him bawling out the gardeners, or trotting his horse in the yard, and I was still aftaid to enter his bedroom without knocking first. Curious, is it not?'

'Very curious, sir,' said the bailiff, regarding him covertly from under the brim of his hat, at the table.

'About the tenants,' said the squire, turning away from the palm. 'I think it might be a good idea if I visited them myself'.

Macneice licked his lips and dropped his eyes. 'There is no need for you to have to do that,' he said. None of this was lost on his employer who noted it and mentally added it to the list of things to attend to, at a later date. Macneice's reaction, when added to his earlier flushing, and his comment about their being 'no need', all spelled out a warning that the man was stealing from him. He smiled and told the bailiff he could go about his work. Daniel Macneice stood up and closed the ledgers with a heavy snap, tucking their bulk under the arm of his leather jerkin.

'Tell the groom to have my mare ready after lunch, and hold yourself in readiness too,' said the squire smoothly. 'You and I will visit all the tenants this afternoon together, and find out why they are behind with their rents. Oh, and close the door after you when you go out please. The temperature and moisture level must be kept constant in here at all times, or the orchids will die.'

Later on, a servant came into the conservatory and announced that the squire had a visitor.

'Who is it, Malcolm?'

'It is your sister, sir, Lady Hood.'

'Peterkin,' she cried swishing through the door held open by the servant, in her silk dress. 'Brother, how good to see you, but I cannot stay longer than ten minutes.'

'In a rush as usual, I see, Rosamund,' he said. Then his eyes widened in open admiration. 'But, I must say that violet becomes you very well. Are you wearing something fashionable, or is that an old dress that I have seen before?'

'I have not come here to discuss my dresses, brother,' she said in a half-whisper, going to look out at the lawns through the bank of glass panes, and fiddling with her kid gloves incessantly. The young man furrowed his brow, for he hated to see her in any kind of distress.

'Rosamund, is something troubling you? Is anything wrong?' he asked.

She turned round and shook her head wildly. 'No. It is just that I may have to go on a long journey, that's all.'

He stood up, going over towards her. 'A journey? Going away? But when? This is the first time you have mentioned such a thing to me. When do you propose to go on this long journey, and where will you go?'

She put her hands up as he came near. 'Please don't touch me,' she entreated him, using her eyes like a tragic actress. 'I cannot tell you anything more at the moment. Only that I must go.'

Peterkin smiled coaxingly. She would tell him soon, he was sure.

It all sounded very mysterious, but he wasn't worried by the news. He was one of the few men who could see what other men saw in his sister, for she was truly a beautiful creature, with her golden hair and deep blue eyes, like the sea lapping against a cornfield in Devon. Rosamund was dressed in her finest, and that too made him think that he need not worry about what she had told him. His sister only dressed up for balls, and masques and happy things she looked forward to with excitement. Only when she was sad or something had gone awry, did she dress down, he knew.

'Well, when are you going? Surely you can tell me that?' he said.

'Could you ring for some coffee?' she asked, turning back to face the lawn through the glass again, and avading him.

'Of course,' he bowed, picking up the silver bell on the table at his elbow and giving it a light shake. The servant came and he ordered coffee for them both. Over the coffee she began talking again, to stop him pestering her with questions of his own, he supposed.

'You have done well since father died,' she said, gazing out over the sunlit grounds from her seat. It was a fine June morning and the sky was very blue and almost cloudless, with the hypnotic drone of bumble bees out in the garden a constant accompaniment to their conversation together.

'You did quite well too,' he reminded her. 'You married a Lord, who conveniently died three months later and left you well provided for. Isn't that so, Rosamund?'

'An impoverished lord,' she laughed humourlessly. 'And what he left me in his will was after all, only my own money, that father had given to him, for my dowry as the   marriage settlement. And my husband was a fine man wasn't he. Over fifty and bald! You never liked him did you Peterkin? You knew as well as I did, that he was like all of the young men who made a nuisance calling here. I was marriageable because I was a Sholto.'

'You haven't touched your coffee, Rosamund.'

'I don't want it, thank you. Anyway, I have to go.'

She stood up and smoothed the creases out of her long violet dress as he watched her with a mixture of sadness and longing. He rose up and leaned on the table talking earnestly. 'Rosamund if you go away I will be desolate. I will pine every day until you return. Worrying about you will make me ill, I tell you. Please set aside any thoughts of making a journey, however long or short. Why do you want so much to go on this long journey, anyway? You haven't told me.'

'I don't want to go, I just have to,' she said, going to the door and lingering there, looking back at him. For all the world as if she was committing every feature of his face to memory. He felt a chill creep across his heart as he watched her in turn.

'Rosamund,' he cried brokenly. 'Rosamund, I forbid you to go on any journey without me, do you understand. I would fear for your safety. A young and attractive woman of means would be prey to all manner of dangers and of men. You will be safe with me, if I go too.'

She smiled sadly.

'Peterkin, you cannot come with me. I wish it were otherwise, but it is not. I have to make this long journey alone, that is all I can say. No, don't touch me. I must go. I am already late.'

He remained where he was, leaning on the conservatory table, half in bright sunshine, half in shadow, and watched her departure in the black carriage until the coach had long gone out of sight through the trees that screened the big house and its long drive from the road, and then he sank down. Laying his head on his hands he sobbed bitterly. A great wall had risen up between a brother and sister who had always been so close till now. Rosamund had changed, or he had, he didn't know which. All he knew was that he adored her more than any other woman alive and she alone, because of her stunning looks and inner beauty, had prevented him from marrying all these years.

The sounds of a furiously galloping horse came to him and he sat upright. Hooves clattered in the yard and he heard someone shouting at Smithers, the groom. Quickly he got up and went to the door opening it and peering out.

Sunlight flashed from the strange horse's harness buckles and its bit, almost dazzling him. Then he saw the vicar, and relaxed. 'Oh, vicar, it's only you,' he quipped. 'I had thought the whole of the King's cavalry had arrived unannounced to share my lunch!'

'Mister Sholto,' said the vicar, an elderly man in a vast powdered wig that showed much neglect, for he was an honest soul. 'Mister Sholto, I have urgent news for you that will not bear any waiting, and you shall hear of it at once.'

'Well then,' smiled the squire. 'What is this news that will not bear any waiting, reverend sir? You must tell me of it immediately.'

'Not here,' said the vicar quickly. 'Somewhere more private sir. For this news strikes at you in an intimate way, and you should be the first to hear of it, before others less kindly disposed to your finer feelings than I am, force you to hear of it last.'

Peterkin Sholto looked at him strangely.

'My finer feelings? You intrigue me vicar. Please come in. I do all my private listening and talking in the conservatory. Let us go there now, and you can unburden yourself of this news that so excites you. Let me precede you, I pray, only the door is stiff and needs an experienced hand to open it without injury to the knuckles. There, please go through and sit down. Coffee, at all? You must be very thirsty on such a hot day, after your fast ride up from the village.'

'Nothing thank you, Mister Sholto. Perhaps a small glass of water afterwards. But first let me tell you what I have come to say.'

'You have just missed my sister Rosamund,' said the squire, as they sat down opposite each other in the temperate atmosphere among the green plants in the orchid house. 'I can only hope that your news will be far less ambiguous than hers was'.

'Your sister, Mister Sholto?' said the vicar in astonishment. 'Did you just say that your sister had been here in the last few minutes, before I called?'

'Yes, indeed I did. Why?'

The old vicar looked very troubled and shook his head from side to side. 'Mister Sholto, that could not be,' he pronounced gravely. 'I know that, because I came here to tell you that your sister Rosamund died very early this morning, in her house at Potlings Bar, over sixty miles away. That was the news I had so urgently to give you. But you look pale. Shall I ring for your servants?'

'No,' replied the ashen-faced younger man. 'What you have said to me vicar. It is impossible. Rosamund was here as large as life. She cannot have died.'

The old cleric shrugged, and laid his quivering hand on the squire's arm. 'Sometimes, we know not how, apparitions come and visit us, to reassure us about something. Your seeing your sister Rosamund must have been one of those. You should feel pleased and grateful to a merciful God that he so honoured you, in this way, my son. Not everybody is granted such a grace, I assure you. Many are left grieving for a loss with no comforts at all. Your sister coming here as she did, in her spirit clothes, was her way no doubt of saying goodbye, as you were as close a brother and sister in life as I have seen. Do not be saddened by this visitation. Or let your heart fill up with great fear of her ghost. It is God's doing, I assure you. Do you understand, son?'

'No,' replied Peterkin Sholto furiously. 'Rosamund was no ghost, but flesh and blood just like you and I, vicar. If she had died, as you say, then I would have known, because we are so close. She was here man, talking just like you and I are now. Why, she even asked for a cup of coffee, so there's your proof.'

The vicar smiled. 'And did she drink the coffee, Squire Sholto?' he asked quietly, probing with his all-seeing grey eyes.

Peterkin dropped his head, shaking it in despair. 'Why, no, she did not,' he said angrily. 'I would that she had. Then she would still have been here when you called just now. Who told you that my sister had died vicar, by the way? It must be a very unhappy person to make up such a wicked thing.'

'No wicked person sir, just the County Coroner's clerk. Mister Sholto, you must brace yourself now, and be a man. Your sister Rosamund had a bad fall from a horse when she was riding by herself, which proved fatal. What is known is this. The horse apparently misjudged a flint wall, and Lady Hood was thrown awkwardly sideways, as it went down. Unfortunately, instead of just banging her head when she struck the wall, she caught her neck on the jagged top surface, and was decapitated - her head completely severed at one blow. One blessing out of this is that it happened so fast that she could not have felt anything. And the horse is unharmed, and without a single scratch.'

Squire Sholto gave a long moan and slumped back in his chair, sliding to the floor of the conservatory. The vicar jumped up and rang energetically for the servants.

Easy Money

'NIFTY TED IS IN YOUR TOWN TODAY' screamed the headline in the local newspaper. Two lads, Bertram and Jack, bought a copy and opened it at the centre page.

There was a photo in a rounded frame of black printer's ink, of a middle-aged man with glasses on, with a pencil moustache and stuck-out ears. Underneath, it said: 'NIFTY TED, AND HE IS IN SEAPORT UNTIL MIDDAY TODAY. IF YOU SPOT HIM ANYWHERE ALONG THE PROMENADE, SIMPLY CHALLENGE HIM WITH THE WORDS: YOU ARE NIFTY TED, I CLAIM MY FIFTY POUND PRIZE FROM THE ECHO.'

'Blimey,' said Jack, 'that's easy money. All we have to do is stop this bloke, and we can earn twenty-five quid each.'

'Cor, yeah,' said Bertram, who was often short of coherent verbal statements.

So the two lads caught a bus to the seafront, and were on the bare and windswept prom at 10 a.m., scouring the immediate area. They made several errors in recognition and went on one tedious wild goose chase when they followed a man in a grey mac into a children's playground. By eleven they were very tired and fed up.

'Where's this Nifty Ted?' demanded Bertram in a petulant tone. 'I thought you said he would be here with fifty pounds, for us.'

'He's supposed to be,' moaned Jack. 'He'll be here somewhere. Skulking behind a newspaper, I'll bet. It will be a *Morning Echo*, Bertie, so look for any bloke on his own, or walking with a woman, who has a copy.'

'A copy of what?' asked Bertram, looking confused.

'The bleeding *Morning Echo*!' said Jack.

'Well, what shall we do then?' asked Bertram.

'You go that way Bert, and I'll take the other side of the road and we'll sweep our way down. That way we can't miss him, you got me?'

Bertram nodded.

'Hang on,' said Jack. 'He will be bound to try and make it a bit of a challenge 'cos if he's too obvious he'd soon get spotted wouldn't he? The newspaper he'll be carrying might be craftily rolled up under his arm, and that sort of thing. Cross over now mate, and if you think you have spotted Nifty Ted, call me, and I'll do the same for you, right?'

'Hang on, Jack. I have forgotten the words. What am I supposed to say again?'

'Just leave things to me,' said Jack, walking off.

A few minutes later, Jack shouted across and pointed at a man near the lighthouse.

'Pull him,' he shouted urgently. 'I think he's the one'.

Bertram approached his prey cautiously. The man was ahead of him, lighting up a cigarette, and cupping his hand to shield the match from the stiff breeze. Bertram sauntered up smiling broadly.

'Hello Nifty Ted,' he said. 'I know it's you. Give me fifty quid.'

'Shove off,' said the man. 'Can't you see I am busy?'

Looking crestfallen, Bertram dawdled back to where Jack was waiting, having just run over.

'Well,' he cried. 'Did he give you the fifty pound prize?'

'No,' said Bertram. 'I asked him for it, but he got annoyed.'

'Did you use the proper words?' demanded Jack. 'Did you say, you are Nifty Ted and I claim my fifty pound prize from the *Echo*?'

'No, nothing like that.'

Jack slapped his forehead in dismay.

'You idiot! You have to say the exact words printed in the paper, or the bloke can legitimately ignore you, and deny who he is.'

'Oh, I get it,' said Bertram.

The man certainly looked the part to Bertram. He had the stuck out ears and the moustache as well and although he wasn't wearing any spectacles he could have removed them, as some kind of impromptu disguise. Where was he now?

'I reckon it is him,' said Jack gravely. 'You just fell down with the wrong challenge that is all. Did he have a *Morning Echo*?'

Bertram nodded uncertainly.

'Yes, I think he had it tucked under his arm, Jack.'

'Right, well, he's on the pier now. I can see him. You go and have another go at him. The fact that he has an *Echo* with him makes him red hot. Go and nab him while I stay here and keep a lookout in case we're wrong.'

The man with the stuck out ears and moustache was leaning on a rail looking out to sea. Bertram crept up and laughed in his ear.

'I know it's you,' he said, 'because of your stuck out ears and the paper under your arm. You can't fool me mate. You are Nifty Ted, aincha?'

'You again, eh?' said the man looking at Bertram. 'Go and play with the traffic and leave me alone. What's the matter? Are you wrong in the head or something?'

Once again Bertram walked away with his head down. Still poor, and still without the twenty-five pounds he had been promised.

'Hey Jack, you're not conning me are you?' he said. 'You told me we'd get fifty pounds and it was easy. But it's twenty past eleven now and we've been here since ten. And that bloke was very insulting to me just now. I think he's getting fed up with me keep going up to him.'

'Relax,' said Jack. 'Did you challenge him correctly?'

'What on earth do you mean?' asked Bertram, puckering his brow into a mass of lines with the effort of thinking.

Jack opened the copy of the *Echo* in a fury and tapped aggressively at the centre page.

'Here are the words, you dummy,' he shouted. 'Look, I'll rip them out for you so you can carry them with you next time. Now, that man you spoke to, I am certain he is Nifty Ted, you got me?'

'Yes, Jack.'

'Well, he is still on the pier. Go back with the words on this bit of paper and walk up to him. Then read from this word for word. Then he can't say you didn't get it right.'

'Okay,' said Bertram heavily, taking the fragment torn from the newspaper.

As he walked up the man's eyes narrowed.

'I'm going to read to you now,' said Bertram happily.

'So read, if it will make your tiny mind happy,' said the man with a sigh.

'Right, I will,' said Bertram, taking a deep breath, and holding the torn out piece of paper in front of him: 'Yesterday in Parliament, the Prime Minister, Mr Tony Blair, said that there were too many farmers evading E.C. quotas....' - Hang on, is that Braxted?'

'Brussels,' said the man.

'Oh, yeah. Have I said enough to get the money yet?'

The man turned away and stared out to sea again looking pained. He lit up another cigarette.

'You had better blow,' he said, without turning round. 'The home will be expecting you.'

Bertram went back to Jack.

'Okay,' said Jack eagerly. 'Hand over my share.'

'It can't be him,' said Bertram miserably. 'I read all about Braxted, but he never batted an eye. Then he said I ought to go home.'

'I'm not altogether surprised,' said Jack glaring hard at him. 'You had the piece of paper round the wrong way, you idiot. You were meant to read the other side to him. The part with the large block capitals.'

'You never said,' said Bertram huffily.

'Never mind,' said Jack. 'We are in luck still. The geezer is where he was, on the pier. Perhaps he likes you and wants you to have another chance to win the prize which is pretty decent. Get over to him again quickly because it's almost twelve, and it's our last chance.'

'Why don't you do it?' said Bertram.

Jack shrugged.

'Well, he knows you,' he said. 'Go on, go up to him again quick. We only have three minutes left because if Nifty Ted isn't recognised by twelve o' clock, the money goes to charity.'

Dragging his large feet reluctantly, Bertram went back to the pier and clumped his way over the wooden planking boards and up to the man with stuck out ears.

The man saw him coming and grimaced as he held onto his trilby hat, for the wind was getting stronger now the sky was overcast and grey. Once more Bertram stood in front of him and held the torn piece of paper up with a smile. The man did not smile back.

'What do you want now?' asked the man in a resigned voice.

'You are Nifty Ted,' said Bertram triumphantly, 'and I claim my fifty pound prize from the *Echo*. There, how about that, and it's not even twelve yet?'

The man fixed him with his eye.

'Come with me,' he said suddenly, taking his arm.

'Can my friend come?' asked Bertram happily. 'After all, he deserves a prize too.'

'You'll do for the moment,' said the man. 'Anyway, there is just the one prize, and you have won it.'

'Can you give me the money in two lots of twenty-five pounds and not too many pennies please,' said Bertram, as the man led him into the arcade.

'No problem,' said the man. 'Just wait here a moment.'

Bertram stood watching the lights go on and off on the pinball machines as the man walked away, dreaming of what he would spend his half of the easy money on.

Meanwhile the man with the stuck out ears and moustache found a patrolling policeman and took him back to the arcade. He pointed at Bertram patiently waiting and oblivious to their presence.

'You see that idiot with the banana-coloured tracksuit and the corks around the brim of his hat, officer?'

'Yes sir.'

'Well, I think he is some kind of pervert, who gets a thrill out of going up to complete strangers, and reading to them. He has been bothering me all the morning. Could you do something about him for me, please?'